Praise for
A Purpose Under Heaven

"Derek Smith has created characters that resonate long after the book has been closed. This allegory tells of the love, loss, anger, jealousy, and shame that tests the faith of families. It also speaks powerfully to hope and redemption."

—Michelle Nunn
Co-founder and CEO, Points of Light & Hands On Network

"The allegory is not dead. In *A Purpose Under Heaven*, Derek Smith revives this venerable story form, infusing it with drama, sadness, humor, and compassion."

—Mary Lou Leary
Executive Director, National Center for Victims of Crime

"In addition to its advantages, technology has the potential to deliver real risk right into our homes and families. *A Purpose Under Heaven* is a page turner that carries us to a moral universe where good ultimately triumphs over evil."

—Rev. Dee Shaffer
Executive Director, Harmony Square Ministry, Brunswick, Georgia

"*A Purpose Under Heaven* is a page-turner that's hard to put down. In less than two hours, you get a sense of just how much technology impacts our lives, and a vivid reminder of the need to stay involved and connected with our family, friends, neighbors, and colleagues."

—Len Pagano
President and CEO, The Safe America Foundation

"With a beautiful narrative style, storyteller Derek Smith shows that while risk envelops today's teens, parents are equipped with powerful tools to steer their kids clear of danger."

—Melanie L. Herman
Executive Director, Nonprofit Risk Management Center

"Easy yet fascinating 'can't put it down' reading! It conveys a deep understanding of human nature and a true feeling for our changing society, under the cover of delightful simplicity. The message is genuine, important and universal. The reader, glued to every page, will become personally enriched by the journey and the experience."

—Dr. Michael J. Kami
World-renowned change strategist

"A *Purpose Under Heaven* is a wonderful allegory that explores the delicate balance between good and evil as influenced by technology. It is a multi-generational story told over time that weaves social, familial, spiritual, and technological issues together like a fine tapestry. A definite must-read."

—Judy Fergusson
President, CEO, and co-founder, Bright Impact, Inc.

"A *Purpose Under Heaven* unfolds in a small American town whose residents are often overwhelmed by the swift tides of dislocation—divorce, single parenting, crime, isolation, and alienation—surging through America today. It examines technology's role in both accelerating and mitigating the risks all of us face."

—William Berger
Chief of Police, Palm City, Florida,
and Past President, International Association of Chiefs of Police

A Purpose
Under Heaven

A Novel

Derek V. Smith

August House Publishers, Inc.
ATLANTA

Published 2008
by August House Publishers, Inc.
3500 Piedmont Road NE, Suite 310
Atlanta, Georgia 30305
404-442-4420
http://www.augusthouse.com

Cover design by Shock Design & Associates

Book design by H. K. Stewart

Manufactured in the United States
10   9   8   7   6   5   4   3   2   1

LIBRARY OF CONGRESS CATALOGING-IN-PUBLICATION DATA

Smith, Derek V.
A purpose under heaven / Derek V. Smith.
p. cm.
ISBN 978-0-87483-853-4 (alk. paper)
1. Technology--Social aspects--Fiction. I. Title.

PS3619.M5813P87 2008
813'.6--dc22
2007031496

To my parents, Don and June Smith, whose kindness, decency, and spiritual faith instilled in me a lifetime of family values. To Lisa, my loving wife, who inspires me with her everyday greatness. To our wonderful children, Hanley and Tanner, who are blessings from God and an expression of the abundance of His love.

Acknowledgments

The act of composing *A Purpose Under Heaven* has been a truly remarkable and inspiring experience. So many passionate, caring people gave generously of their time and talents. I am particularly grateful to the following individuals for their encouragement, feedback and contributions:

A community of readers including David Davis, Carol DiBattiste, Ansley Jones-Colby, Dr. Ricardo Martinez, Mary Helen Moses, Bill and Pat Neuenschwander, Michael Reene, Russ and Melanie Richards, Reverend Dee Shaffer, and Julie Zimbardi, who embraced the storyline and provided insights, experiences, and suggestions that brought enhanced relevancy and clarity.

Laurie Shock, for a cover design that graphically depicts the dynamic tension between technology, humanity, and spirituality.

Graham Anthony and August House, for their faith in the power of storytelling to entertain and educate, and for invaluable market experience.

Leah Williamson, my Executive Assistant, whose dedication and professionalism set a standard of excellence I admire and appreciate.

Reverends John and Judy Wolfe, whose spiritual faith is an energetic example of the grace of God's love and a beacon of light to so many.

Mike Kami, my mentor and friend, whose call for a better world through global compassion and technological innovation has become my privilege to communicate and passion to advance.

Liz Parkhurst, editor and advisor, whose wise counsel, steadfast support, and professional touch transformed the manuscript with patience and skill.

Vince Coppola, my co-writer and friend, whose amazing talents brought conversations, commentary, and philosophies together through characters that taught me the value of family and community, and that within each of us lies a force for good.

Preface

A *Purpose Under Heaven* is my attempt to generate a discussion about one of our society's great challenges: the unrelenting, exponential growth of technology and our capacity to deal with its consequences. I've created an allegory because in a world of short attention spans and endless diversions, a good yarn can entertain and still communicate meaning.

Today, life feels unsettled. Time appears to be speeding up, everything happening faster and faster. The very nature of change, once tied to the seasons or the rhythmic turning of the tides, has changed, becoming sudden and erratic. We try to cope as we search for meaning and answers in a technology-driven, ever-changing world. Some respond with denial, seeming to take pride in avoiding if not renunciating newly available tools; most of us, though, accommodate those changes with a gnawing sense of anxiety and dread.

Our lives move so quickly that it seems the future has arrived ahead of schedule. It often does. Despite the marvelous technology—the communications, information, and medical breakthroughs all around us—few of us feel confident or in control.

The traditional institutions that nurture us—family, school, and place of worship—are themselves being redefined by technology. We no longer have to be at home, in school, or at church to communicate, learn, or seek spiritual nourishment. However, this comes at a cost: too often we forgo the benefits of face-to-face communication, companionship, or worship.

Today, a paradox confronts us. As scientific breakthroughs create new capabilities and endless possibilities, we experience a corresponding decline in insight, understanding, and ethical behavior. Don't blame the machine. Technology is amoral. It will inevitably reflect—and magnify—the value set of its users. Therefore, our leaders—educators, communicators, medical researchers, yes, even our clergy—must be steeped in technology *and* enlightened social policy. Today, few have been trained in this holistic perspective.

The paradox is particularly apparent among families, especially across generations. Our youth, technologically savvy, often are socially challenged. They struggle with face-to-face conversations and direct human interaction, more comfortable hiding behind electronic shorthand, hoping to shield their insecurities and emotional vulnerabilities. They are just beginning to comprehend the delicate balance between friendship and community in technology-enabled social networks and the dangers and future consequences of scattering one's image, emotions, and innermost thoughts in cyberspace. Much education and personal reflection are needed.

Conversely, our seniors, quick to embrace an unhurried talk, handshake, or hug, often are technologically challenged. Not wanting to appear incompetent, many of them reject technology's opportunities to instantly communicate, follow family activities, or research breakthroughs in medical technology. Seniors willing to participate in a wired world are vulnerable to scam artists and schemers wanting to exploit their trust and good nature. Ongoing technological support is critical and must be made easily accessible.

It is ironic that the basic skills needed to be shared for thriving in our complex world reside within the extended family. We have a unique opportunity to share and transfer knowledge within the family unit to the benefit of all.

These are just a few of the issues pulsing beneath the surface of *A Purpose Under Heaven*. Feisty Nana Martin, her family, friends, and neighbors, Pastor Richards—even the dreaded Pale Man—are personifications, but they are not abstractions.

Their days and weeks are packed with the routines of real life. They experience love and loss, anger, jealousy, and shame. They strive and succeed or fail; they suffer setbacks, disappointments, and moments of selflessness and sacrifice. They are vulnerable. Their faith is tested and shaken and rekindled. They exhibit the callow concerns of youth and the regrets and frustrations of old age. They have the ability to endure and mature.

In short, these are recognizable human beings forced, like all of us, to live in the dizzy gap created by galloping technology and our inability to keep pace. Personally, I believe destiny does not lie in the stars or our imperfect genetics. It is humanity and compassion—God-given virtues—that give life meaning and purpose.

If you are facing some of these issues, if you see yourself or your family staring back at you from these pages, I invite you to read on, start a dialogue, and join the conversation.

—Derek V. Smith
Cashiers, North Carolina

Prologue

My name is Ephraim Richards, Pastor Emeritus at New Hope's All Hallows Church. I turned ninety-four this year, well beyond my biblical portion of three score and ten, beyond even those hearty men blessed to see four score.

Over the long years of my ministry one truth resounds: we draw strength and solace from our belief in the existence of a benevolent Divinity. The world's religions also recognize the existence of an opposing force, resistant to the purity of God's love, dark to the light of His saving grace, vengeful and tormented to His joy. I name this force the Pale Man.

This story recounts what began one long-ago spring. Whether it be truth, the product of an old preacher's failing memory and overzealous imagination, or a parable that resonates as strongly today as it did in my small town a generation ago, I can no longer say with clarity. Extend a courtesy to an old man. Read on, decide for yourself.

Chapter 1

I buried Erma Gabriel this morning. She was the last of our faithful group. My hands trembled as I read the service to the handful of mourners gathered at the gravesite, and not just with age. I sensed something in the trees, watching. There was a hush in the air. Birds stopped chirping; squirrels stood immobile as statues. I heard urgent whispers, a mocking laugh that must have been the wind. I grew lightheaded, not unusual for a man of my years. Someone steadied me. I shivered in the unseasonable heat.

Has the Pale Man returned? Is the wolf once again circling my flock?

The old fears are flooding back, and yes, the old strength: "Yea, though I walk through the valley of the shadow of death, I will fear no evil; for Thou art with me."

I sense my time grows short. I confess my heart flutters against my breast. But I will not rest until the story is told.

I cannot rest.

Fifteen years have now run their swift course. Dom Palermo, Dorrie Smith, Sam and Rose Stone, Joe Adams, Bob Gabriel and now his wife, Erma, and dear Nana—bless her soul—have gone to their reward. May they rest in glory. Their children and grandchildren have moved on, pursuing dreams in other places, hopefully carrying the best of our community with them.

Like Ishmael, I alone am left to tell the tale.

A knock. Mrs. Brown is at the door with my lunch. She imagines me an old man, Methuselah in a backwards collar, dozing at an antique computer while the cobwebs collect inside my head.

Bless her heart, but I do not sleep. When my tale is done, I believe you will grasp the meaning of the events that unfolded in New Hope those many years ago.

And my purpose will be fulfilled.

This is Nana Martin's story—I'm merely the messenger—but it reveals a universal truth: like God's grace, parental responsibility and love are timeless and all-encompassing, the seeds from which all good things in this life take root.

* * *

As the afternoon sun streams through the rectory's stained glass windows, I find myself returning to another spring at the turn of the twenty-first century. Even then I wasn't a young man. I'd been pastor at New Hope's All Hallows Church for thirty years when Nana Martin retired.

You wouldn't remember New Hope. It was never a place that called attention to itself, certainly not a place where one would expect momentous things to occur. New Hope was a small town like many American towns, familiar and fading in the dawn of a new century, a timeless place with whitewashed churches and an oak-lined square perfect for a stroll on warm Saturday nights.

By the way, my computer's name is George, a faithful companion as ancient as I. Pastor Richards may be slipping, but George still has quite a memory.

It began slowly, but the signs were everywhere. The dramatic, nationwide decrease in violent crime of the previous decade had begun to reverse itself. Our schools were becoming warehouses for disaffected and often overmedicated children. Our economy, and thus our livelihoods, seemed uncertain. The sense of purpose that so recently defined our nation was giving way to discord and animosity. Public discourse was bitter and acrimonious. We were distrustful of each other, our leaders and institutions. Such an environment emboldens those of ill will.

* * *

I remember a sparkling morning. I'd visited a young couple whose wedding was a few weeks away. They'd been so busy with caterers and invitations and such that the immensity of the commitment they were about to make finally struck them. They wanted counseling and assurance. I believe I helped them, for they are still married and leading a class on parenting at All Hallows.

Afterward I decided to head over to the Elite Diner to grab a bite.

(Lord, how I miss Dom's cooking.) On Main Street, I noticed the shoe factory's tower decorated with bunting and a crowd gathered on the sidewalk. Considering the tough times, this certainly drew my attention. I walked closer. A banner—NANA MARTIN ENJOY YOUR RETIREMENT!—was draped over the rail.

There she was! Dress red as a candy apple, silver hair coiffed, sensible shoes. I caught a whiff of her perfume; it reminded me of gardenias and church services on Sunday mornings. Generous with her smile ... distracted.

You'd think Nana would be happy to retire after so many years keeping Bob Gabriel's books, tracking every invoice and expenditure like it was her own money. She'd raised a family. Her faith was strong, her commitments steadfast. She'd contributed in a thousand ways—bake sales and charity drives, volunteer work at the hospital, singing in the choir—to make New Hope a shining city on a hill, an ideal that often shimmers beyond our reach.

You would be wrong. Change was in the air. Not gentle zephyrs but tumultuous change, unpredictable as a summer storm.

Her family—Nana's greatest joy—had become her great concern. She loved her daughter, Jane, and her granddaughters, Rachel and Sarah, fiercely, sheltered and shielded them like a mother bear, but as she grew older, the burden of this responsibility began to wear her down. Jane was a loving mom, but her ideas on parenting confounded and frustrated Nana. It was more than old versus new approaches. It was the difference between ideal and real, between security and risk that multiplied like a virus. Jane had encouraged her girls to be curious and open, ignoring the risks and temptations every child encounters.

Jane lived in a luminous bubble of well-being. Trust was vital; distrust opened the door to the isolation and depression affecting so many single parents. She embraced the new people and ideas pouring into New Hope as surely as Nana feared being swept away. Rachel and Sarah lived a sugar-and-spice idyll Jane had created to offset the uncertainties of adolescence and a vanished father. There were no wolves or witches in this fairy tale.

These fears were bubbling inside Nana that morning. I'd felt tingles of uncertainty myself; many of us did. These were years when the foundations of small-town life were being uprooted, creating new rules we were slow to embrace:

Not everyone means well.
Strangers are not friends you haven't yet met.
Everyday life carries a burden of risk.

A Holocaust survivor once visited our church, a messenger whose suffering and strength touched our souls. Nana lived by his words: "Once you bring life into the world, you must protect it." Who would protect her family when she was gone? Values did not flow like pond ripples across the generations.

Over the years, I've prayed over another question. Did Nana's dilemma, familiar to so many parents, somehow echo beyond New Hope? Did it draw attention on a higher plane of existence? Was a larger battle being joined? In a season of faith, the truth conveyed in the Gospel of Matthew is obvious: "Are not two sparrows sold for a farthing? and one of them shall not fall on the ground without your Father's notice."

In the beginning, I was too caught up in the busyness of ordinary life to appreciate such possibilities. I loved to mount the pulpit, thrilled to the majesty of my own words, and exulted in the fact that All Hallows contributed more to charities and did more volunteer work than our sister churches. Sound familiar? As Proverbs warns, "Pride goeth before destruction, and a haughty spirit before a fall."

Yes, New Hope had been blessed. We imagined such blessings would continue to fall like cherry blossoms in spring. Instead, we were tested. Innocence is a beacon. I believe evil had begun encircling us like the coils of a snake. And temptation, cunningly clothed in everyday dreams and desires.

Yes, I speak of the Pale Man. Is he real or a figment of my imagination, the stuff of unsettled dreams? I confess I still cannot say, and on that glorious spring day, who would have believed me?

Chapter 2

The sun was high in the sky. Birds were singing in the trees.

The crowd parted as I drew closer. A few congregants who'd been skipping services slipped away to avoid my gaze. Nana smiled at me as she made her way up the stairs to a makeshift stage, nodding to co-workers on the rails. Bob Gabriel, president of Well-Heeled Shoes, stood waiting at the podium. We applauded as Gabriel proclaimed:

"Motherhood, grandmotherhood, and a successful career have earned our Louise a well-deserved rest ..."

Once started, old Bob could go on longer than a Jesus-loving, devil-hating preacher at a revival.

"... In the old days, I'd have presented a gold watch," he said five minutes later, reaching for a box wrapped in ribbon and gilt. "Times have changed. I say we must change with the times."

All of us strained to see as Nana undid the wrapping. Was it sunlight that flashed on the sleek, laptop computer she held? Light that glinted like cold fire. I didn't know much about computers, but this was something special; it thrummed with power and promise. Nana looked at it doubtfully, as if she'd been handed Aladdin's Lamp without instructions.

"Yes siree, ordered it put together special," Gabriel went on. "It does Internet and video and ... all kinds of stuff!"

Bob, no spring chicken, didn't have a clue about this machine. Actually, no one did.

Nana stared for a moment, then rubbed her hands together.

"Open Sesame!" she joked.

Nothing. She winked at Sarah standing alongside Jane and Rachel at the foot of the stairs.

"Open Poppyseed!"

We laughed.

"Did you say Internet?" Nana made it sound like a bad word. "What about these Greeks I read about?"

19

"Geeks, Momma!" Jane called out.

"Oh."

A ripple of laughter spread through the crowd.

"Greeks ... Geeks," she shrugged, poking the machine. "Beware of Greeks bearing gifts."

"Excuse me," said Bob. "My mother happens to be Dutch."

Anything that wasn't familiar as an old shoe made Nana uneasy. Back then, computers made my generation uncomfortable—well, not uncomfortable as much as uncertain. Not everybody, mind you. Some folks took the new technology in stride, probably the same ones who had jumped right away to VCRs and microwaves. The rest of us felt this Information Highway had passed our exit by. The Internet was for young people. We didn't understand that a computer was a tool, a switch that allowed us to connect to our families and children and friends no matter how far they'd drifted. There was a directness to technology, a yes-or-no quality, that quickly pierced the veil of pretense; it made good relationships stronger, yet exposed and laid bare those that were false or frail. We didn't understand any of this, and so we felt like maybe our cares, our hopes, and yes, our loneliness, didn't count for much.

Bless her heart, Nana was curious. At Sunday school, she'd fire scriptural questions left and right, giving me—and I excelled at exegesis—all I could handle. She could be stubborn when she put her mind to something. As a child, Louise—that was her given name—was always ready for a challenge. Jump off the high dive, climb the oak tree behind Jimmy Miller's house when the rest of us held back. I appreciated that side of Nana. She was special. Maybe that's why she was chosen.

Chosen is a big word to drop into a conversation. Bear with an old man who wanders and sometimes mixes past with present, the real and the ephemeral. I believe you'll see what I mean.

Well, Nana was going on about geeks as Jane and the girls stepped up to the podium. The kids mugged and raised their granny's arms over her head like she was a champion. Right then,

I remember this skinny photographer, all dressed in black, walked up and began shooting pictures. He went on and on, the camera's shutter clattering like an old lawn mower until Dom Palermo, who ran the town's oldest diner, grumbled, "How's about giving it a rest, buddy?"

The guy gave Dom a look.

Nana and Bob reminisced about all the good years, and Bob shed a few tears. We knew the factory was in trouble, but outsourcing was something few of us really understood. Bob, who'd inherited the business from his father, had spent too many days on the tennis courts when maybe he should have been responding to global competition. Turned out some guy in Vietnam who didn't know a volley from a lob was running a shoe factory that cost us jobs in New Hope and lots of other places.

The laptop shimmered. Rachel and Sarah could not take their eyes off it. While Nana was talking, Bob nodded and Jane pressed the ON button on the side of the machine. The thing popped open like a clamshell.

"Hello, Nana. I'm George."

The genie had come out of the lamp. "It's alive!" Sarah teased.

Everyone else was laughing and shaking their heads. Bob beckoned me to the podium. Not one to miss an opportunity to do the Lord's work, I thanked everyone for the great success of the spring charity drive and told them I expected to see just as many of them on Sunday. I sang a few bars of "May the Lord Bless You and Keep You." The crowd joined in. I saw tears glistening in Dom's eyes.

Later, we ate the rich chocolate cake—shaped like a boot— Dorrie Smith, Nana's best friend, had baked. Folks told stories about the good old days, their words floating like a child's bright balloons into the perfumed air.

Chapter 3

I keep a scrapbook. You know what I'm talking about—old-fashioned paper photographs, wedding and birth announcements, obituaries, clippings from the *New Hope Courier*—a comfort to a man who's the last leaf on the tree. When I thumb through the yellowing pages, I'm carried back.

The good old days were drawing to a close. New Hope's old families were slowly disappearing. Workers were being let go at the factory. Like I said, Bob had waited too long to invest in technology or merge or do *something* to keep Well-Heeled Shoes competitive.

Maybe I'm being hard on him. Would anyone in a small town back then have really believed global events—not wars or regime changes but subtle things like labor costs or technical innovations—could have such an impact on our well-being? You had to look hard, or you'd miss what was happening. Out on the Causeway, a sparkling mall was crowded with shoppers, but the lights in the old shops on Main Street were winking out. A new car sat in front of every home. A parade of new people was moving in and out of town, in some cases before the ivy in the front yards could take root, while our own young marrieds, unable to afford the soaring real estate prices, moved away.

Jane Martin thought the newcomers brought a breath of fresh air to a community too stifling for her tastes. That's interesting, because the families who stayed and became part of our community said that's what they *liked* about New Hope.

There I go, starting to wander.

Dorrie, Nana, and the other church ladies had a welcoming committee. I'd usually join them—you know, meet and greet the new neighbors. We'd go knocking on doors with baskets of fruit, one of Dorrie's fabulous cakes, some church literature.

Some doors should have had DO NOT DISTURB! signs on them. It didn't take long to realize some people were hungry for things besides faith, fellowship, or neighborliness. They'd lost sight of the values that sustained us and fantasized about the latest, greatest experience, you know, Ferrari cars or vacations in Fiji. I'd glimpse them in their mini-mansions staring at make-believe lives on flat-screen televisions. They were puzzled when their shiny toys left them unhappy. After a bit, they'd move on to the next town, the next job or marriage, disappointed but still searching.

The Tragedy that had struck the City a few years earlier hung over us, obscuring the threat in our backyard. I still preach over how blind humans can be and how quickly darkness can take root. And people still stare at each other uneasily.

Pastor Richards has gone round the bend, they think.

I smile because they're a loving congregation.

Nana's retirement party was the last carefree day we would have for a long time. The lengthening shadows veiled an evil as real as these four walls. Yet, we were not alone. I sensed a divine essence also at work. Who or what would prevail? Isn't this the eternal battle? Or is our fate, so to speak, faithless, simply an accumulation of everyday choices? This is for each of us to decide, though I confess I made my choice long ago.

Chapter 4

Nana Martin was a widow. She'd been married to Jack Martin. Jack and I grew up together, played baseball and football at New Hope High. We were drafted right out of school. It was God's will that we survived. Afterward, when I could no longer ignore the voice crying out to me, I went into the seminary. A few years after my ordination, I went back to the Pacific, not as a warrior but a preacher spreading the Word. A decade later, wracked by recurrent bouts of malaria, I returned to New Hope.

In 1951, Nana and Jack were married at All Hallows. Seven years his junior, Nana often joked that she was a "child bride." They stayed married thirty-five years. Jack, Nana, Dorrie, Dom, and the rest of us were part of what they call the "Greatest Generation," but we never knew it. We did what we were supposed to do to the extent that we were able—went to work, raised families, struggled to give the kids better opportunities then we'd had. We loved our country, though not in the chest-thumping way you sometimes see. Loved it as a beacon of light and hope for the world.

As young men, Jack and I played softball on summer afternoons. He drank a beer or three, enjoyed poker games on Friday nights with Dorrie Smith's husband, Don, George Simms, and the rest, grilled hot dogs in the backyard for his wife and daughter on the Fourth of July. Jack attended church most Sundays. If he didn't, the man couldn't look me in the eye, and the following Sunday, there'd be a little extra in the collection plate.

Jack worked in a garage off Main Street. Eventually, he bought the shop and built a good business until the Pep Boys, NAPAs, and Econo-Lubes with the ten-minute oil changes began circling like sharks. He refused a good offer to open a transmission franchise. Jack was a stubborn man, maybe foolishly so. He said he didn't want any partners telling him what to do. He wanted to stay independent.

When things got bad, he tried harder, scrubbing customers' windows with a squeegee when they bought gas. He reminded me of those battered fighters who keep answering the bell long after the bout is lost. Jack believed he was invincible, believed working harder and putting in longer hours would pull him through. He was wrong, and Nana took a job at the factory to help keep the family afloat.

Jack smoked, a habit lots of us picked up during the war and couldn't shake. He was up to three packs a day when he lost the garage. He quit smoking when he was fifty; by then he was hacking and gasping. "Emphysema," Doc Stone told him. Things went downhill: oxygen tanks, a walker, ambulances, and emergency rooms.

Sam Stone and I were there when he died. The scene is etched in my memory so vividly I could reach out and ... Nana gripped his hand so tight. She begged him not to leave. With his dying breath, Jack said he had to go and swore he'd look after her as long as she lived.

I *believed* Jack Martin.

Excuse me. I must fetch a tissue from the box Mrs. Brown keeps in my desk. Is it odd that a man aches for the people and things—a song or a particular fragrance can pierce the veil of time like a spear—he loved when he was young?

I see myself as a simple man, God's fool determined to do His bidding. Thomas Aquinas wrote, "To one who has faith, no explanation is necessary." Can a spirit cross the great divide that holds us separate and apart from the love and joys, cares and suffering of this world? I confess I do not know.

Chapter 5

Two months have passed since Nana's retirement party. She's in her office going over bills, though it's not an office as much as a family album with walls. Photos, awards, and children's drawings cover every inch of space. Molly, a Labrador retriever, is asleep at Nana's feet, snapping at flies in her dreams. Nana does her calculations by hand, making checkbook entries with a ballpoint pen, ignoring George blinking atop her desk. Rosemary Clooney's "Tenderly" whispers on the radio, carrying her on the wings of memory.

She catches part of a news bulletin and sits up.

"… Jones, a volunteer at All Hallows Church, allegedly embezzled five thousand dollars in contributions, money earmarked for a youth summer camp. A spokesman for the New Hope Police Department revealed Jones, who moved to New Hope two years ago, has a criminal history. More troubling allegations may be emerging ..."

"Mike Jones?" Nana says. "All Hallows?"

All Hallows is our church. Mike Jones was my responsibility, though I confess my first impulse when I learned of the embezzlement was to shout, "There's nothing I could have done." Isn't that the case when something goes wrong on our watch? I trusted Mike, praised him when he volunteered for this fundraiser and that outreach, assumed he was an honest man. Isn't that the Christian thing to do?

I was too busy to notice that Mike had lost his way. He betrayed my trust, but I let my congregation down. I believe God will forgive me. My God is a merciful God. I, on the other hand, have had a much harder time forgiving myself.

In the office, Nana shakes her head.

"Can't be."

The Joneses live around the block. She can see their house from her window. If she closes her eyes, she can see Sarah, red hair flying, playing soccer with April Jones in the backyard. No, Sarah is in school. Sarah is fine. Sarah is safe.

Sarah is ... what?

Nana doesn't know. She hates not knowing. She picks up the phone, starts to dial, then realizes she doesn't know whom to call. She turns up the radio volume, but the broadcaster has moved on. Nana tries another station and another.

Unease is flowing like ice water in her veins when a shrill beep startles her—George. She looks at the computer as if seeing it for the first time. She's watched Jane and the girls jump on and off for weeks, sending e-mail, doing research, getting movie times and weather reports, reading the newspapers, downloading (whatever that is) songs on "Eye-toons." Watched but never paid attention.

George is no different from the DVD recorder Nana could never program, or Jane's cell phone camera, more trouble than it's worth. She did like the glow from George's screen. He made a cheap lamp.

Nana was suspicious of technology. She came of age in the 1950s, when the threat of nuclear war was part of every school-girl's catechism. In her lifetime, technology had birthed the gas-guzzling behemoths that crowded the highways, and fuel more expensive than perfume. Technology had given us abortion and "designer drugs" with no thought of consequence. Criminals and terrorists were subverting technology in ways unimaginable in the confident years after the fall of the Soviet Union.

Nana's attitudes were typical of millions of Americans. The medical miracles of the twentieth century—the eradication of smallpox, the development of the polio vaccine, the advances in the war on cancer, the hybrid crops feeding billions of people— were taken for granted. Nana was also wary of "Big Brother," though she couldn't rightly say who he was. She certainly didn't want computers snooping around like Martha Evans, her busy-body neighbor.

Until now. She stares at George's screen, hesitates, fingers on the keyboard.

"Okay," she says and hits ENTER.

George hums. His screen glows bright, revealing a series of multi-colored little signs. Puzzled, Nana reaches for the "mouse" she's seen Sarah handle comfortably as a glove and clicks on one, then another. Screens come and go, images flash and disappear with dizzying speed. Finally, she notices a voice-activation doohickey and clicks HELP.

"*Pergo, tactus numerus duos!*" George booms.

"What the heck! You don't speak English, but you speak ... Latin?"

She taps the keyboard. "*Inglese.* English."

George screen flashes. Text begins to flow in English.

"That's better. Mike Jones."

The screen flashes again. A window appears.

"Google? Are you making a joke? What the heck is Google?"

Nana clears her throat. "Search Michael Jones."

She types MICHAEL JONES into a box on the screen.

Instantly, dozens of Michael Joneses parade, screen after screen, in front of her eyes. Car dealers, musicians, auto-repair-shop owners, high school athletes, a seventeenth-century pirate, insurance salesmen, stockbrokers, roofers, lawyers, small-town mayors, and a member of Canada's Parliament. So many Michael Joneses, there might as well be none.

"Too many. Am I doing it wrong?"

The computer is silent. She taps the keyboard impatiently, considers giving George a thump, then worries she'll damage the uncooperative lump.

Nana clicks the mouse. Nothing.

"That's it."

She folds George like a waffle iron, presses the OFF button. He squawks about not being "shut down properly."

"How about working properly?"

Nana glances out the window at the picket fence that marks Mike Jones's backyard. She sighs and removes George's instruction manual from a drawer. For the next hour, she reads and takes notes.

She looks up when she hears Sarah slamming the front door shut and shrieking when Molly rushes to lick her face. Sweet music.

Chapter 6

Jane Martin drives past Romper-Rhymer Child Care, taking in the crowd of toddlers in the playground. Romper, operated by a chain in the City, competes head-to-head with Jane's Happy Kids day-care center. The bright, airy building ("An Award-Winning design") surrounded by emerald turf is so appealing it ties a knot in Jane's stomach. She's lost half-a-dozen kids and can't afford to lose more. Actually, she's lost the parents to glitzy advertising and the power of America's bigger, newer, brighter fascinations.

A photographer stands outside the playground snapping pictures of the older children, no doubt, Jane imagines, for a wonderful newspaper story.

"It's not how much you spend," Jane says aloud. "It's how much you care. No, too long. Let's see. Happy Kids We Care. No."

Jane is a believer. She believes people—her ex-husband the exception—mean well, though she suspects that the franchisers who run Romper-Rhymer treat children like fast food: herd them, process them, wrap them in glitzy packaging, ignoring the unique needs of individual kids. She believes, or at least believed, that competition would be a good thing, a chance to show what Happy Kids could do. How naïve was that!

She even believed Andy Stevens, New Hope's fastest-talking real estate broker, when he told her he'd sold the Romper property to a chain that ran senior citizens' homes—and then had the nerve to ask her on a date.

"Andy, you creep!" she shouts into the hot, empty street.

That summer, Jane turned thirty-eight, still "bubbly and bright as a new penny" (to quote her high school yearbook). She sees herself as a spiritual person, though often too busy to make church. Maybe too embarrassed. In New Hope, divorce is less common than in the big cities—and more of a stigma.

Jane does care. She loves her little charges and sees perfection in a child's openness. She believes "childlike" was humanity's natural state until we bit the apple and encountered guilt and sin.

Jane is juggling things—children, career, finances, her personal life, and an aging parent. She's always running—what mother isn't?—but not moving forward emotionally or spiritually. Is she overlooking lessons others have learned so painfully? Like many single moms, Jane is lonely and hurting behind her brave front.

When she was in college, a professor convinced Jane that evil was aberrant behavior, an illness resulting from nature or nurture gone astray, not, as the Scriptures say, the work of souls who've rejected God's saving grace. A decade later, a young theologian—I'd invited him to preach at All Hallows—convinced Jane that Hell is "the absence of God."

"And the devil?" Jane asked.

"Merely a fable."

All this is buzzing behind Jane's clear eyes and sunny demeanor as she negotiates Main Street's traffic. She turns on the radio, flips the channels. The station Nana has been listening to is now reporting a robbery at a retirement home.

"... the well-dressed intruder apparently got by security guards by pretending ..."

She mashes the OFF button. Bad news depresses her.

"Why don't they report the good things that happen every day?"

She's loaded *Teach Yourself French!* onto her iPod and listens as the introductory music filters through the car's sound system. That's more like it. Jane hopes to fly to Switzerland next winter to improve her skiing, maybe meet Monsieur Right. She begins the repetitive drill.

"*La neige est belle aujourd'hui.*"

"The snow is beautiful today."

She visualizes crystal mountains under an ice-blue sky.

"*La neige est belle aujourd'hui.*"

She's on her way to pick up Sarah at ballet class, drop her off, then head back to Happy Kids before the parents show up; then it's home for dinner and overseeing the girls' homework.

"La neige n'est pas belle aujourd'hui!" she sighs. *"Mais non!"*

She parks the car in front of New Hope École de Ballet. Breathless, she jogs up the steps and nods at a tall, oddly dressed woman stapling a sign—DANCING ON THE EDGE/STUDENTS WANTED—to a cork bulletin board.

Jane introduces herself.

The woman's name is Shelby. Jane, who rarely meets artsy types, is bubbling with curiosity. Shelby is a dance therapist. Her partner, Gerro, is a performance artist specializing in "astral dance." They're new in town, eager to meet people, get this avant-garde dance class up and running, maybe scout some talented youngsters for the dance companies in the City.

"The artist's life is struggle ..." says Shelby.

"... and full of contradictions!" exclaims Jane. She's pleased to remember the line from a class she took in college.

"You got it."

"You're really going to open another dance studio in New Hope?"

"Gerro sees opportunities."

"Opportunities? I don't know about that."

"Sure there are."

"Really? What are you looking for?"

"Me? The usual things—fame, fortune, and my own TV series!"

Both women laugh. They chat a few more minutes. A few of the girls from Sarah's class come skipping down the stairs.

Jane hesitates then blurts, "Maybe you could meet my older daughter, Rachel. She wants to dance. She's a cheerleader, almost as tall as you. Maybe give some advice. It's better coming from a professional"—Jane makes quotation marks in the air with her fingers—"than Mommy."

"Is she serious about her craft?"

"Serious and very eager."

"She should definitely meet Gerro. He's got connections."

"That's been the problem. There's no one around here for her to reach out to. Her gym teacher? No way! Miss Jenkins upstairs teaching ballet for twenty-five years? I don't think so. Everyone else is a soccer mom, good mother, dutiful wife, totally status quo. You know what I mean?"

"Maybe. Though you really can't tell what's churning beneath the surface. Nothing is what it seems. Maybe your friends are trying to hold it together. Maybe they're struggling in their marriages, hoping things will get better. Maybe they owe a lot of money on the mortgage. Or their husband just got laid off. I don't know, an autistic kid. Maybe deep down they hate soccer, Brownie Packs, and S'mores. I bet half these women are working hard to do the right thing, to keep their kids from making some stupid mistake that will haunt them for the rest of their lives."

"Right," says Jane uncertainly.

"I'm not saying it's going to work out for them. It's just ..."

"What?"

"Nothing." Shelby takes a deep breath, turns back to the bulletin board. "I sure wish my mother had tried harder."

Jane stares at her. This conversation is more *real* than she bargained for.

"I'm trying," Jane says meekly.

Introspection makes Jane uncomfortable, especially coming from a total stranger who seems so together.

"Maybe we all could do dinner?" Jane offers. "I'd love to bring Rachel along."

"Rachel," says Shelby. "Such a pretty name. It's from the Bible, right?"

"Right," says Jane. "But we're not super-religious."

"You know, young people really fascinate Gerro. He loves their energy and openness ... How they're so comfortable with computers and stuff. It's a mutual thing. Teens find him magnetic."

"He sounds awesome. You're lucky."

"Yeah."

There's something else going on. Jane craves Rachel's respect, and she's convinced the quick way to earn it is to treat the sixteen-year-old as an adult. Have her take ownership and make some decisions. Not on everything, of course. An artsy friend like Shelby might be a bridge.

Shelby stares at Jane as if reading her mind.

"Believe me, you're not the first parent to approach us for guidance. I think I can speak for Gerro. We'll be happy to audition Rachel. If she's got the talent and desire and we hit it off, we'll go forward. Mentor her if that's what you really want. *C'est cela?*"

"*Oui, merci!*" Jane grasps Shelby's hand. "This makes me feel so much better. I can't tell you how I stress over that girl. I want her to be happy."

"That's what we do," Shelby says. Again she looks into Jane's eyes, unsettling her.

"How about you? Are you comfortable in your own skin? Are you centered? I sense you're struggling. You know, astral dance is an amazing relaxation technique."

"Really?"

"Take a deep breath." Shelby places her hands on Jane's shoulders. "Don't be afraid."

"I'm not."

Self-consciously, Jane closes her eyes, takes a breath, and is startled to find her eyes brimming with tears. No one has been this sensitive in years, and this, this stranger is staring straight into her soul. Forget the fact she's never heard of astral dance.

They walk out of the building chatting like old friends. On the sidewalk, Shelby does something else to reinforce Jane's belief in the kindness of strangers, the belief that good things will happen if you're open. She says she'd be willing to teach creative movement at Happy Kids as a volunteer.

"Really? Our parents will love it! I ... I'm not sure how I can compensate you."

"Not to worry. I try to give back when I can."

"Wow. That's so great."

Jane is beginning to compose a slogan when Sarah rushes up in her leotard and ballet slippers.

"A natural redhead!" says Shelby. "How cool is that?"

Jane makes a quick introduction. Sarah nods and grins.

"Thanks," Sarah says, brightening. "I get a lot of teasing, you know."

Chapter 7

Rachel Martin skips onto New Hope High's athletic field. On the sideline, Jamie Kaufmann, the "hottie" senior quarterback, stands laughing with Dottie ("Snotty") Rice, the cheerleader captain. Rachel puts her head down and walks faster. Not fast enough to miss Snotty's smirk.

"Not fair!" Rachel thinks. "Why is she always the chosen one?"

Across the field, Joe Adams is making his rounds, patrolling the parking lot, shooing dawdling students onto departing buses, a routine he's followed for decades. He has always been a disciplinarian committed to earning the trust placed in him by parents and the school board. Like many disciplinarians, he's toughest on himself and his family. With Adams as principal, the school has grown stronger academically, successful athletically, and, knock on wood, relatively free of the drugs and disciplinary problems afflicting so many other schools. Joe has paid a price. His wife left him years ago, and now his son ...

He walks across the field's lush green carpet. The "Adams bounce," the distinct stride parodied by generations of students, is gone from his step. He takes a seat in the bleachers behind two freshmen puzzling over an algebra assignment. The kids melt away.

The bogey man, Adams thinks as he pulls a sheet of notepaper and a pen from his jacket pocket. He unfolds the paper, stares at the words.

Colleagues and Friends:

This is not an easy letter to write. I've tried many times to find the words to explain. I ...

Pen poised over the paper, Adams becomes aware that a man wearing sunglasses, creased pants, and a black silk jacket is sitting next to him. The man has a camera bag over his shoulder. Adams shoves the resignation letter into his pocket.

"Joe Adams?" the guy says, extending his hand. "Roger DeWalt, Digital Harvest."

Adams blinks. "Sorry. We don't do purchasing at the school. You need to talk to the district office."

"Relax," the man says, patting Adams's shoulder. "I'm not selling anything." He pauses. "I do recruiting—IT, mostly. That's where all the action is. Today, I'm just a guy enjoying a sunny day in a pretty town. Don't you love the smell of fresh-cut grass?"

Adams says nothing.

"Can't let any grow under our feet, now can we?" DeWalt chuckles.

Adams's face is blank. DeWalt tries again.

"I'm a guy who keeps my eyes open for opportunities. Who doesn't? In fact, I've been talking to some people. I hear good things about you, Joe. You run a very tight ship. No slack. No nonsense. That's leadership, you ask me. A rare commodity."

"Thanks." Adams can't think of anything else to say.

Sensing Adams's discomfort, DeWalt shifts gears. "The weather always this warm?"

"It'll get cold."

"So I'm told. Joe, I'm going to be evaluating prospects over the next couple of months. I'll be honest. If you decide to leave education, let me know first. There's interest out there in a guy like you. A good man is a scarce commodity. What are you, fifty-two? Today, that's young. We could make things happen."

"I've no interest."

"Heard that one before. The question is, what do you want? What's your objective? Financial security? I don't see a problem. Travel? Perks? Escape the old routine. What's it, twenty years you've been working here? Got your pension all squared away. That's good."

He removes his sunglasses, mops his brow with a handkerchief.

Adams is silent.

"Whew! Hot. We could talk over dinner if you like?" He fiddles with the camera bag. He pauses, stares at Adams's stone-face.

"What do you say? Let's grab a drink tonight. Expense account, you know." He pats his jacket pocket. You can fill me in on things in New Hope."

Things are not good. Adams has not slept, not really, in ... he doesn't know how long. Joe Adams won't see Doc Stone. He keeps things in. That's his nature. Be strong, keep your emotions hidden, set the example. On his desk is a plaque inscribed with a quotation from the *Canterbury Tales*: "*If gold rusts, what will iron do?*"

Joe's hand closes around another letter in his pocket: "*The Secretary of Defense regrets to inform you ...*"

Steve killed in combat. Twenty-one years old, his only son. The pain comes surging back. He fights not to sob in front of this stranger. He's on his feet, trying to clear his head.

"You must excuse me," he blurts. "I'm not ... I'm ..."

A whisper. "I knew him."

"What!" Adams spins around.

"You drove him off."

The sky, the clouds begin to pinwheel.

"What did you say?"

The shout in Joe's throat is choked back to a whimper.

"I was about to suggest we have ..."

Adams backs away from the bleacher, stumbles, catches himself.

"Careful."

DeWalt pulls a camera from his case. He appears oblivious to Adams's distress. "I'd like a picture for my files: *Joe Adams, Educator*. That says it all. The light's perfect. I want the school, too."

"I ..." Adams remembers something in his office. He wants to go there desperately.

"Won't take a sec."

On the field, cheerleading coach Alice Watters is jogging over to talk to Adams about a scheduling conflict when she sees him having his picture taken by some sort of photographer. What's that about?

"None of your beeswax, Alice," she reminds herself and turns back to her girls.

She doesn't see Adams hurrying away.

DeWalt begins snapping pictures of the cheerleaders with a telephoto lens.

On the sideline, Rachel notices him, steps forward, and poses, all pouty, like the girls she sees in MTV videos. Now the man is completely focused on her, the shutter clattering as he shoots, one, two, half-a-dozen images, drawing Watters's attention. She approaches, again thinks better of it. Her whistle shrills. The man frowns and lowers his camera.

"Rachel Martin! Over here! Now!"

"Rachel Martin," the man whispers. "Such a pretty name."

Chapter 8

Nana is at her desk, glasses perched on her nose, studying George's manual, gingerly pressing keys, nodding at the lightning responses. She leans back, gazes out the window. Dust motes dance in the sunlight. She drifts as the radio whispers.

> *... To everything—turn, turn, turn.*
> *There is a season—turn, turn, turn.*
> *And a time to every purpose under heaven ...*

She's between waking and dreaming, certain she's about to grasp some life-altering insight or intuition. Sure enough, the phone jangles.

"Darn it!"

It's a broker saying he has a client who wants to buy her house, a rambling Victorian that's been in Nana's family a hundred years. Not a good idea. Nana's loyalty to place—even if that place has drafty windows and creaky stairs—is intense. Her house is home base, the bear cave.

"Are you trying to fast-talk a senior citizen?" she rumbles. "You tell Andy Stevens Louise Martin isn't going anywhere. That pest has been after me since my Jack passed."

George's screen flickers. Nana adds that Andy Stevens would con a widow out of her last dollar and then climb over her to grab the front pew in church.

Everybody knew Andy, what with him slapping his picture on the side of buses and appearing on TV shouting "Big Andy Comes in Handy!" He should have been selling used cars out on the Causeway, but he went on to become the biggest developer in the area. Never gave a nickel to the church. If he hadn't suffered a massive heart attack in his forties, Andy would have probably built himself the biggest mausoleum in the cemetery. Dom Palermo joked that Andy was probably selling timeshares in Hell.

The agent realizes Big Andy's lead ("an old widow eager to sell—jump on her") is not gold-plated. He blurts goodbye and hangs up.

To everything—turn, turn, turn.
There is a season—turn, turn, turn.
And a time to every purpose under heaven.
… A time of war, a time of peace,
a time of love, a time of hate …

The haunting lines from Ecclesiastes echo in Nana's head long after the deejay has moved on. Too long. With a start, Nana realizes George has recorded the song and is playing it back. Son of a gun! She waggles her finger at the computer.

"Had me going, didn't you?"

Chapter 9

Nana, like Joe Adams, keeps things to herself. She doesn't tell anyone that her robust health is turning. She'd suffered bouts of dizziness and shortness of breath. A recurring dream—a creature pale as bleached bone lurking in New Hope—is troubling her sleep. She worries constantly about Rachel and Sarah. News reports about the harm suffered by children at the hands of trusted family members and acquaintances fueled her fears, as did television programs highlighting the vulnerability of children communicating on-line.

The girls are forever whispering on the phone, constantly fiddling with the new computer and who knew what other gadgets. She can't keep track of them all. Seems like that darn Information Highway ran right through the Martin household.

A week later at Temptation Mall, her unease blossoms into full-scale panic.

Dom Palermo told me the story. Nana, Jane, and the girls had gone shopping. The mall, with its automated People Movers, interactive advertising kiosks, throbbing music, and towering video displays, was the proving ground for a number of startling innovations. Shoppers could make purchases in a department store or pay for a burrito at the authentic Mexican restaurant using their cell phones to log onto a secure network that instantaneously identified them and debited their bank accounts.

The mall had turned the sleepy suburbs outside New Hope into a hive of activity that drew thousands of people on the weekends. Overwhelmingly, these were families, teenagers, and eager shoppers, but concealed among them a were handful of criminals and predators eager to exploit new territory.

The moment they'd arrived Rachel rushed off to a cybercafé offering wireless Internet service. Jane ducked into Nordstrom's to return a blouse. Sarah vanished while Nana was distracted by an animated video display.

Five years younger than Rachel, Sarah was still the baby in the household and enjoyed the role thoroughly. I always thought Sarah, with her sprinkle of freckles and coppery ringlets, symbolized youth's evanescent purity, a girl who made people smile or shake their heads as they recalled their own childhoods.

Like Rachel, Sarah craved the spotlight, and that made her vulnerable. Rachel knew right from wrong, understood limits and boundaries and still crossed the line, often deciding rules did not apply to her. Sarah was old enough to know better, but Sarah, like many overindulged children, was self-absorbed and impulsive.

Dom Palermo, strolling through the mall with his eight-year-old grandson, Nicky, spotted Sarah in the gigantic Pet Emporium playing with the puppies. Not a clerk or customer was in sight, a situation that instantly reminded Dom of the kidnapping and murder of a four-year-old Florida boy more than twenty years before, a tragedy that had haunted Dom for most of his own son's—DJ's—childhood. He gripped Nicky's hand tighter.

"Sarah?"

"Hi, Mr. Palermo."

"Are you here by yourself?"

"No, I'm with Nana and Mom. Rachel's around somewhere too."

"I meant here, in this store. Does Nana know where you are?"

"Mom says I'm old enough to look out for myself."

"Really? Why don't we go find them? Sarah, why don't you hold Nicky's hand? He's wearing my arm out."

* * *

They walked and walked until Dom spotted Nana. Imagine her terror. She looked so pale Dom considered calling the EMTs for assistance. She'd been walking around for twenty minutes and couldn't find a policeman. Nana didn't notice the emergency call boxes scattered around the mall, didn't realize there were child-monitoring mechanisms and alert systems in place all around her. All she knew was that Sarah was gone.

When Jane finally showed up, she gave Sarah a two-minute lecture then nodded her head in satisfaction as if to say, "See, good parenting is not such a difficult deal." Nana started to express an old-fashioned approach to handling the situation, something to do with grounding and suspended privileges. Sarah became "defensive." Jane insisted that Nana was being "insensitive." Nana shut her mouth.

Dom bought ice cream cones for everybody. Driving home, Jane declared the incident a "learning experience." She'd already convinced herself that Nana had overreacted. Because it ended well, Sarah's risky behavior—as so often is the case—was forgotten by everyone but Nana.

Chapter 10

The next day Dom calls to check in on Nana. He knew how panicked she'd been at the mall. Nicky had given him a good scare once or twice. Dom loves to tell stories; he tells Nana about the computer DJ gave him for his birthday.

"... Imagine my kid telling me it was time I modernized my bookkeeping and inventory! Said there were spreadsheets in there. I couldn't find no sheets, just pillows. That's a joke. Right now, the thing is in the back, sitting on a case of pork and beans. Next time you drop by, maybe you could give me a few pointers, being an expert and all?"

"You know," says Nana, brightening, "I really don't think it's hard. What I'm doing, e-mail and reading the paper, is pretty straightforward."

"I know about them e-mails. You type in a lot of little letters, like a secret code. Right?"

"Dom, there are no secrets. Take a class. That's what I'm going to do. The school is right up the block from the diner."

"You think? My fingers are too fat. I keep hittin' two, three keys at once."

Dom's fingers weren't too fat. His head was, God bless him. Computers were less complicated than his special tomato sauce. Back then, you could buy a book, figure out next week's weather, visit the Louvre, pay your bills, learn the latest health-care information, and a million other things. Yet, the majority of senior citizens—myself included—never touched a computer.

Dom hangs up as the lunchtime crowd starts to arrive.

Nana yawns and stretches, closing the manual on her lap. Her gaze moves to a black and white photograph: a soldier, tanned and lanky, smoking alongside a World War II Sherman tank. She's reminded of an old achingly painful pop song, "Forever Young."

It was taken on Peleliu Island in October 1944. The photo is on my wall now. Look closely, and you can make out "Ol' Faithful" painted on the turret. That was my idea.

Another photo sits on Nana's desk, faded with time. Her mother hovers alongside as Nana takes her first ride on a two-wheeler. Three children run shouting behind. Neighbors smile encouragement. Nana flashes a devil-may-care smile.

The reverie ends with a slam of the front door. Seconds later, Sarah rushes into the office, drops her book bag, and takes a macaroon from a tin Nana keeps on the desk. She squirms as Nana tries to plant a kiss on her cheek.

"I'm too old for that stuff!"

"Never too old. I've got a present for you," Nana says. "Belonged to my mother."

"Horse and wagon?" says Sarah. "A dinosaur?"

"Come here, wiseacre."

Nana removes a crucifix on a thin silver chain from her desk. She slips it over Sarah's head. When Sarah steps back to look in a mirror, Nana ruffles the top of her curly mop.

"Thanks!" Sarah smiles at her reflection. "Will it protect me from Dracula?"

"God will protect you. Nana will be right behind."

"Does God have a behind?" says Sarah, chuckling at her own joke.

"You know, I don't know."

"Nana, can I play a game?"

"You can if you know how. I can't figure that kind of stuff out yet."

She's reaching for George's instruction manual when Sarah wiggles alongside her in the chair.

"Ouch!" Nana grunts, but her heart soars. "I learned how to do e-mail!"

"That's easy! Let me show you this new game. You put these on." She hands Nana a pair of odd-looking goggles she pulls out of the desk drawer.

"You know how to do 'www.dot,' right?"

"Right." Nana's not sure.

Sarah's fingers race across the keyboard. A moment later, a three-dimensional image of a Tyrannosaurus Rex charges out of George's screen. A deafening roar fills the room. Nana jumps back. Sarah laughs in delight. Nana reaches to touch the beast, then catches herself.

"Isn't that something!" she marvels, pulling off the goggles.

"ISN'T THAT SOMETHING!" mimics George.

"There he goes, being silly."

"George isn't silly," Sarah says. "He's actually pretty darn smart!"

Chapter 11

Nana's brown Buick rolls down Main Street. She's oblivious to the honking SUV a foot behind her rear bumper. Nana parks and gets out, carrying a pair of shoes. She drops a coin in the meter and disappears among the passersby. She stops at Nick's Shoe Repair ... or what used to be Nick's. Nick's is gone, replaced by Soleil, a boutique.

Rose's Dress Shop, Johnny's Butcher Shoppe, and Peterson's Dry Cleaners are also missing. In their place, the Leaf & Bean, Level 3 Digital Academy, and Walter's, a café serving lunch "al fresco."

She spends the next hour in Level 3's introductory class, taking notes until her eyes are strained and her head buzzes with programs, search engines, and such. The search engine thing amazes her. In ten minutes, she's located Emily Dyer, her best friend who'd moved away in the eighth grade. She sends "Em" an e-mail. E-mail certainly comes in handy; since Mike, her mail carrier, retired, it takes three days to send a letter across town.

Compared with George, the Level 3 computers are slow and, well, impersonal. After class, her instructor, Manny, a tech whiz from India, salutes Nana as his "most hard-working pupil." Beaming, she drops her rhinestone reading glasses in her purse and heads out the door.

She walks up Main Street. It's hot. She sits on a bench hoping for a breeze. The trees the town council planted a few years back have bloomed into a lovely canopy. She mops her brow with a lace handkerchief.

"You okay?" asks the man next to her.

"So humid," she says, fanning herself. She'd swear the bench was empty a moment ago.

The man pulls a leather bag open and fiddles with a camera. "Mind if I make your picture? I collect interesting faces."

"Thank you, no. We haven't met, I'm sure."

"Roger DeWalt. I'm working with Joe Adams."

"Mrs. Jack Martin. Joe is a good friend."

"Then how about a picture? See, I've got Joe right here in living color."

"I don't think so."

"I know you. You're in the computer class. A little old for video games, aren't we, Louise?"

"I'm not there to play games."

"Games can be fun." DeWalt gets up, folds his jacket across his arm. "Then if you'll excuse me."

"How do you know my name?"

"Is this Twenty Questions?" He walks off.

Nana looks down, spots the red HELLO MY NAME IS LOUISE tag pinned to her blouse.

"Wake up, Louise!" she grumbles.

She pulls the tag off, feeling her privacy has been invaded. A moment later, a wave of nausea passes over her. Gasping, she steadies herself, and it passes. She waves off a passerby's offer of help. She looks around. The sun is shining, pedestrians chat on their cell phones, two sparrows chatter on the branch above her head. She feels as if the world has wobbled then righted itself.

"Lord," she whispers. "What's happening to me?"

She decides to get her eyes checked. She's been staring at computer screens too long. She sits back down, forces herself to breathe slowly and regularly until she feels better.

Twenty minutes later, she walks up Main Street to the Elite Diner. Dom and the regulars are shooting the breeze at a long table across from the cash register.

"Well, look who's here!" Dom shouts. The regulars nod and call out greetings. Nana straightens up and smiles.

"Thought you were gonna come by and help me with you-know-what," Dom says. "I did something wrong?"

"You, Dom? No way."

"You're getting skinny," says one of the women.

"I wish." Nana stares at her reflection on the mirrored wall. Pale, yes. Skinny? No way.

"What'll it be?" Dom asks Nana. "Whiskey?"

"Orange juice." She sits down.

"On the rocks?"

"Squeezed."

"Squeezed! Coming right up. Hey, I got that thing in the back."

The conversation is as familiar as the patty melts Dom has been serving for twenty years. Traffic ... sports ... politics ... gossip. Who died, who was born, who's getting divorced, newcomers who don't care a lick about their neighbors.

Dom hands Nana her juice. After a minute, he takes her elbow and leads her to the back of the restaurant. A man sits in the last booth, face buried in a magazine, a camera bag at his feet. Dom ignores him.

"I meant what I said about coming around. Don't be a stranger." He lowers his voice. "I'm feeling kinda down. I meant to tell you the other day. Me and DJ, all of a sudden, we got this failure to communicate. Started with the business. He wants to expand, open another diner over in Greenport, maybe a couple more down the line. I don't know. Sounded pretty risky. Borrowing a bunch of money and all. Know what I mean?"

Nana nods.

"We used to go to ballgames together," Dom says. "I'd fix Sunday dinner for him and Sally. No more. Yeah, we talk and all, but we never say anything. Know what I mean? It's like these kids walking down Main Street always blabbing into their cell phones, never saying anything. I know he's married and all, but there's no more 'Hey Dad, you want to drive into the City for a game?' No heart-to-heart conversations. Forget about it! 'Busy ... busy ... busy.' The windup is I don't get to see Nicky. I don't get to be a part of the family. Don't want to sound like a crybaby, but I tell you, sometimes ..." He takes a deep breath. "Know what I mean?"

"Tell me about it," a guy says, passing on his way to the restroom.

Startled, Dom grouses, "Can we get a little privacy around here?"

Dom walks Nana back to the table. The man in the back booth looks up from his newspaper and stares at their backs.

The talk at the table has turned downbeat, what with layoffs and money problems and all the rest. Dom listens for a moment.

"Can we change the channel once in a while?" he says. "Jeez, you guys are depressing."

"Ought to name the town False Hope," Freddie Calder says.

"Lost Hope," grumbles a guy recently laid off at the factory.

"That's it! Don't you guys gotta be somewhere? It's not like I'm getting rich entertaining you."

"Dom, can you freshen my coffee?"

"Sure, Freddie, I got nothing better to do." Dom makes a fist. "Would you like one lump or two?"

Nana knows how Dom feels about DJ. She can't communicate with Jane. Lately, it seems the gap separating the generations keeps getting wider. Like Dom, Nana was big on family values long before the politicians and the preachers grabbed ahold of it and turned it into an issue rather than a prescription for living.

Dom would never tell anyone besides Nana that DJ was planning to open another diner with an outside investor. This wise-guy investor had suggested DJ finance his part of the deal using the Elite as equity. Dom was crushed and then outraged. Like his father, "Big Dom," before him, Dominic had invested his life in the store. All of a sudden his flesh and blood is undermining it? No, Dom can't say that.

"Lemme go grab that computer."

He scoots, apron strings flying, into the kitchen and comes back with a laptop. He plops it in front of Nana like a plate of lasagna.

"I been doing a little homework," he says. "Well, very little."

He fiddles, presses a few keys. Up pops a series of digital photos of Nicky's First Communion. Dom is beaming so much you'd think the boy was standing in front of him.

"How do you like them apples?"

"Actually it's a PC," says Nana.

They laugh. Like they've got some secret that the rest of the gang doesn't know anything about.

"Tell you something funny," says Dom. "I typed in some recipes, but I can't get them out. It's stuck or something."

"You have an e-mail address?" says Nana.

"Yeah," he says uncertainly. "It's DomA@elitediner.com. DJ got it for me. But I don't know how ..."

"I do," says Nana. "Write it down. I'll send you something."

"Don't send me none of them viruses. The Board of Health inspectors are on top of me already."

The tin bell Dom nailed to the door tinkles, and Dorrie Smith stomps into the restaurant. She walks past Nana to Terry, our local patrolman, who's sitting in his favorite spot reading the newspaper. Only it's not Terry. It's a different officer, John Stanley, young enough to be Terry's grandson. She hesitates. Holding a handful of papers, she stands there, hands trembling.

Dom sits her down at a table near the cash register and fixes her a cup of tea. A moment later, Dorrie begins to talk, at first to Dom and Nana and then, unconsciously, to everyone in the restaurant.

For twenty-five years, a percentage of her teacher's salary had been deducted each month and matched by the school board and invested in a pension plan. To her delight, her contributions, interest, and matching funds had grown into a very tidy pile, enough for a widow to enjoy her golden years.

The trouble began a year ago when the county commission decided the fees for managing the pensions of the hundred or so active and retired teachers were excessive, and "opted out" of the business. Dorrie received a thick packet in the mail containing a bewildering number of IRA plans and instructions on how to "roll over" her pension funds to avoid tax liabilities or penalties. This advice might have been written in Aramaic for all the sense it made.

After supper one night, she sharpened a pencil and sat down to fill out the forms. Two hours later, she was still sitting there, unable to decide among money market and mutual funds, no load, tax deferred, or annuities. The unfamiliar terms upset her. What if she made a mistake? After two nights, Dorrie gave up.

When the financial planner—he'd gotten the names of all the county retirees—called to offer his services, she signed right up. A few days later, she arrived at this plush office on the second floor of the New Hope Savings and Loan. The walls were covered with degrees, awards, and community service plaques. She filled out some forms—visions of "no-load funds" (whatever they were) and double-digit returns dancing in her head. She had her bank send the man a cashier's check for $237,000. It was good to have a certified professional working for her.

In three months, the value of her funds had shot up more than ten percent. Six months later (i.e., two weeks ago), driving down Main Street, Dorrie noticed a FOR RENT sign in her financial planner's window.

She parked her car and, heart pounding, ran up to the second floor. The office, completely gutted, was being renovated for another client, a marketing company out of the City. The property manager had no forwarding address for her financial planner.

By then, Dorrie was in a panic. A few days later, her neighbor Clement Garrison—his son was a CPA in the City—told her and the half-dozen other teachers who'd signed on with the same planner, that it looked like they'd been victimized by a fraudulent scheme. It was a police matter.

"How could I have known?" Dorrie asks. She stands, extends her arms as if to include everyone. "He seemed like an honest man. So professional."

No one ventures an answer.

It was the right question asked at the wrong time. Obviously, most financial planners, like most people, are trustworthy. This guy was not. How does one know? Dorrie and the others didn't do anything wrong, not by the standards they'd lived by all their lives. They put their trust in the familiar. The office above the bank, the man's polished and professional demeanor, the pinstripe suits, and the degrees and charitable awards on the walls signified honesty and respectability. But the world had changed. The con man understood their vulnerabilities and took advantage. Dorrie was unaware that there were quick and reliable ways to check out his background and credentials. He played on our eternal frailty, the temptation of easy money.

"The worst crooks always seem like honest men," says Dom, walking over and putting his arm around Dorrie. "You hear about this all the time nowadays. You don't know who to trust."

"What are you talking about?" asks Nana.

"Everything and everybody."

Dorrie's been running around frantically, and nobody knows what to tell her. It's not like she could walk into the New Hope Savings and Loan and talk to Jim Robinson, the president, personally like in the old days.

Jimmy is long retired. A bigger bank in the City, and then another, had swallowed up New Hope Savings and Loan. Dom says if you take away the fancy office, the fake awards, and the fast talk, her "financial planner" is a common thief. Only guys like him are not stealing checks out of mailboxes. They've gotten smarter, using technology like everybody else. Why wouldn't they?

He walks Dorrie back over to John Stanley, the young cop, and introduces them. Officer Stanley, who means well and is very polite, is no help. He's not equipped to handle identity crime. As it turned out, neither were the two detectives down at the station house Dorrie had talked to the week before. Who would they arrest? Officer Stanley hesitates then suggests Dorrie contact Miles Howard, the hotshot consumer reporter on Channel 5.

"That's what I'd do."

"Great. Now we're relying on TV to protect us," grumbles Dom. "Dorrie, you've got to have some kind of insurance. Am I right?"

"No, there's nothing."

The officer's radio squawks, and he's off to a fender-bender out on the Causeway.

"Terry would have done something!" Dorrie calls after him.

Actually, Terry was enjoying his pension in New Port Richey, his badge replaced by a deep-sea fishing rod. It's not like a mugger had grabbed Dorrie's purse in New Hope Park. You couldn't sit back and expect the authorities or the government to protect your retirement or whatever else it was bad guys were plundering.

"A lot of stuff you've got to look out for yourself," Dom says after a while.

Dorrie Smith, helpless. She'd been voted New Hope High School's Teacher of the Year half-a-dozen times. She'd been New Hope's activist, stirring things up, writing noisy letters to the newspaper, supporting this or that wild-eyed candidate. Bless her soul, she'd done missionary work in El Salvador. When she came back, she criticized my sermons as too "middle-of-the-road."

Now, she'd lost her voice and her hard-earned retirement. Dorrie didn't have a cell phone or computer, things that had been around for years but never seemed useful, never mind indispensable. She could have researched financial planners on-line. She missed her grandchildren, but the DVDs her daughter sent her—birthday parties, recitals, T-ball games—sat idle on her kitchen counter. A BlackBerry was something Dorrie bought at the fruit stand up at the lake. At that moment, her horizons, always so expansive, were collapsing like a telescope lens.

"Sit for a minute," says Nana.

"I can't. You don't understand!"

"I want to help. Come by later, and we'll see if George can help. At least direct you to the right people."

"George?" says Dorrie, waving her papers. "Who's George? Besides, I don't have a clue where this guy is."

"He's ... it's a computer. The girls call him George. Silly nickname."

"Dom, what's your computer's name?" one of the guys shouts. "Frank?"

"And beans!" Somebody else answers.

Dom shakes his head. "One of these days you mutts are going to drive me right out of here. This is serious."

"We're kidding!"

It was serious, like somebody had come in and changed the rules. Of course, you didn't know your banker any more than you knew your kid's Little League coach or scout troop leader. Any more than I really knew Mike Jones when he showed up and volunteered. But it wasn't somebody or the government or some corporation Dorrie could blame for the uncertainty she was feeling. There were millions of Dorries out there. It was some *thing*—the breakdown of the extended family and the rootlessness of American culture. It was globalization; it was technology: satellite phones, high-speed networks, whatever, driving all these changes, uprooting traditions and institutions everywhere, right down to tiny places like New Hope.

"It's not just the money, Nana. I could lose my house."

In tears, Dorrie heads for the door.

"Dorrie, wait!" Nana says. "It's going to be okay. I promise you. We'll put our heads together, all of us, figure something out."

She's already up, limping as she follows her friend outside.

Chapter 12

I was unsettled. I couldn't put my finger on what was troubling me. Something wrong with the air, the way the light seemed lifeless and flat. People walked down Main Street with their eyes staring straight ahead or fixed on the sidewalk as if avoiding contact. It's a hard thing to put into words, but familiar things seemed unfamiliar: the newspaper boy riding his bike down the block or the postman making his rounds. It was strangely quiet as if the birds had stopped singing. Even the shouts of the boys playing touch football in the schoolyard seemed muted.

Or so it appeared. I spoke to Nana about this. I asked if she sensed anything unusual or odd. She looked at me a moment but stayed silent. We spent a few minutes making small talk. I couldn't shake the feeling something was wrong.

"How are you doing?" I asked. "Is anything bothering you? Anything you want to talk about? I'm here, you know."

She surprised me with her answer. "Pastor, everyone has a cross to bear."

"Even Jesus accepted help. There's no shame."

I remember she seemed fragile. In fact, Nana had been en route to Sam Stone's office the afternoon Dorrie walked into the Elite Diner.

Sam Stone, M.D. was the man to see when you were out of sorts. A good man though, in my opinion, a stubborn one. Over the years, Sam and I had debated everything from stem cells and euthanasia to evolution to the existence of the soul.

A week later, Nana shows up at Sam's office. He keeps it simple, asks questions, takes notes—the basics. He listens to Nana's heart and has Rose draw some blood. He asks about Jane and the girls, all the while observing her with a practiced eye.

"Okay, what am I missing?"

"Nothing, Sam. I'm maybe a bit under the weather."

"Something's going around."

"That must be it."

He steps out of the examining room to look in on another patient. Nana checks the Band-aid on her forearm and reaches for her purse. She bumps into Sam coming back through the door.

"What's the rush?"

"Off to class."

"Class? Exercise?"

"Computer class."

"What's that about?"

"Never too old to learn …"

"I agree." He takes Nana's hand, looks closely at a spot on her wrist. "Benign. Are you taking your medication?"

"Regularly."

"Regular is good. What's bothering you?"

"No one thing more than anything else."

"Ah, the joys of aging."

He scribbles a note. "Call or stop by in a few days. We'll have your labs." He checks his watch, decides he can chat a few more minutes. Sam loved to well … pontificate.

"You know, I get more and more diagnostic results on-line. It's great. We've got these secure intranets that connect the labs, hospitals, and us practitioners. It's cheaper, quicker, and totally reliable. Now, let me say that's very different from what I usually see on the Internet. Most of that stuff is a bunch of hooey, electronic junk mail, quacks peddling miracle cures. 'Grow hair. Lose weight. Don't exercise! Live longer! Eat bacon and eggs every day!' For research purposes, I stick to the medical journals."

"They're probably on-line too. There's lots of interesting stuff on-line."

"I'm old school."

Nana was not old school, not anymore. It hadn't taken long for her to appreciate the power that technology had put at her fingertips, the gift of knowledge, the ability to communicate what she felt and learned and cared about to the ends of the earth, should she choose, the access she suddenly had to other lives, ideas, thoughts, and dreams.

After class, she'd rush home to George, eager to apply what she'd learned. Only the laptop did things Nana could not find in the class manuals. It anticipated commands and had a built-in personality like those electronic chess sets that laugh when you make a bad move. It had a sense of humor, albeit a lousy one to Nana's thinking.

George's humor never did improve. And he hasn't "spoken" in years. I suspect he chooses silence. We've grown old together, but my understanding of George is still evolving. From the moment Bob Gabriel presented George to Nana, the computer could do much more than search the Internet. It could do things that elevate this story beyond an old man's reminiscence. To this day, I imagine a spark embedded in his memory that makes him unique.

Chapter 13

"Anemic?"

"Afraid so."

Sam Stone tells Nana her blood tests indicated low hemoglobin levels, a condition that can trigger weakness and fatigue. He'll need further studies and more precise tests before he can make a proper diagnosis. His words come to Nana as a whisper she must strain to hear, and in that whisper, an intimation of mortality.

"Can you do the tests?"

"It's better if I refer you to an internist. In this area, diagnosis is almost completely automated, a computer interprets the lab results."

"Really."

Sam again examines her forearms for telltale bruising and other indicators of an underlying disorder. When he's done he confesses to Nana that he too is taking a class, an Asian cooking class at the local college.

"Those are on-line too," she says. "Straight from Taiwan."

"Really."

Rose interrupts before Sam gets into his recipe for Steamed Lobster with Ginger.

"You've got a half-dozen people waiting. You've got to be out of here by four P.M. to see Mrs. Williams on the other side of town."

"So I'll skip lunch."

"You already did. Maybe you should skip some house calls."

"No can do. Maybe you can fix something special for a late supper?"

"No can do. As wife, office manager, nurse, and former bottle washer, I'm advising you that our kitchen closes at eight P.M. Try to get home."

They've had this discussion a hundred times. He refers Nana to a group of internists on the Causeway.

"You know them?"

"Bright young doctors. Technologically superior." He waggles his dented stethoscope at her. "What could be bad?"

"Easy for you to say," Nana retorts.

"Medicine is science on the march."

"Marching over people like us." She pauses. "Not everyone, mind you. Some."

"Some is too many. At the moment, all I can do is change your oil, see if all your sparkplugs are firing."

"Is there a warranty?"

"Seventy-eight years and rising."

"I'm getting close."

"By the way, Janie needs to come in for a physical. She's way overdue."

"You're joking."

"What's the joke? I delivered her, so I'm responsible."

"No, she's irresponsible. That's the problem. Sam, remember how Jack wouldn't come into the delivery room?"

"Jack was squeamish."

They keep this up until Rose physically pushes Sam into the next examining room and sends Nana on her way.

Sam didn't tell Nana that his malpractice premium had just doubled for the third time in five years. His insurance agent told Sam he could pay or risk a lawsuit—every doctor's nightmare—that could destroy his practice. Sam threw up his hands in disgust. He'd never been sued in forty years.

"Times have changed," the agent said.

As he was leaving—Sam's check in his pocket—the agent said he knew two doctors finishing residencies in the City who'd be happy to buy into his practice as junior partners.

"These are good physicians," the guy said, looking at Sam's battered cabinets, "who understand how to run a practice."

"You mean an assembly line? No thanks."

"Sam, you can't provide quality medical care if you can't pay your bills."

"That's my problem."

Outside, the agent, who's heard it all before, mumbles, "Stubborn son of gun."

Malpractice? Stone was the doctor who showed up, for gosh sakes, in the middle of the night when the baby was running a high fever and you were edging toward panic and filling the bathtub with ice water.

He saved this sinner's life fifteen years ago when my heart began clanging like a cheap alarm clock. Generations of New Hope families relied on Doc Stone for vaccinations, penicillin shots, setting bones, fighting ear infections, not to mention his endless store of kindness and common sense.

Sam was thinking of retiring. He was becoming a gatekeeper for the hospitals and insurance companies. He was the one who had to look a patient in the eye and say, "Coverage has been denied." The one forced to consign too many elderly patients to too many "affordable" nursing homes that left much to be desired. He hadn't put his frustration into words but sensed many of his colleagues felt the same way.

In the blink of an eye, it seemed medicine had moved from a healing art to a business. Back then, many physicians could examine a slide and distinguish three different kinds of white blood cells, producing three different kinds of interferon, but didn't know the first thing about comforting a dying patient. Too many physicians were never taught to *listen* to their patients' needs and desires.

I'm being harsh. Many medical schools were training skilled *and* caring practitioners, but soaring costs, insurance, technological innovations like PET scans and MRIs, and government cutbacks were forcing many doctors to see thirty or forty patients a day. And so a gap was developing between the marvels of medical science and a patient's need for human interaction, a need just as important as medical technology.

Fortunately, this chasm has been bridged. We humans do reverse many of the problems we create for ourselves. Today's doctors are true caregivers. Sam Stone would be pleased.

Chapter 14

The morning clouds are clearing. Mrs. Brown and the church ladies are planning to drive the old pastor up to the lake. I imagine them packing picnic baskets with potato salad and ham. Hot apple cider and a checkered napkin to tuck under my chin. Mountain Lake is a special place, a reservoir of both joy and sorrow.

I do love the autumn leaves and how the light turns the water to molten silver, a river of forgetfulness. I should like a nap by the shore but not for long.

Sam Stone's dilemma was a symbol of the upheaval around us. It was created, for the most part, by our inability to comprehend so many changes, occurring so rapidly. It left us uncertain and confused, with little time to react before the next wave broke over us.

We were spectators to our own lives. We turned inward. Few of us were confident enough to stand up and say what he or she felt or feared, hoped for, or believed in. Like Joe Adams, Nana, and Dom, we kept our fears hidden. We didn't open our hearts even to friends. We were not comfortable expressing deep feelings. Was this pride, stubborn independence, or a deeper insecurity? We stayed solitary and alone, our silence crying out in the wilderness.

Perhaps we played into the Pale Man's hands.

Chapter 15

I've suggested the Pale Man might be a fantasy figure invented by susceptible minds like the mass psychosis that gripped Salem, Massachusetts during the seventeenth-century witch trials. I've mentioned he might be a modern construct, a scapegoat for our unwillingness to take responsibility for our actions.

But if the Pale Man is real, was it fate, free will, or the Lord who thrust Nana Martin in his path? That's for you to decide.

As I've said, I believe New Hope wasn't the first.

I believe the Pale Man arrived in New Hope to test the ripeness of our chaotic world and dash our hopes of salvation.

I believe these were the terms of the battle that raged in New Hope. The Pale Man would triumph or be defeated and forced to move on.

Chapter 16

Nana takes a pamphlet—WHAT IS ANEMIA?—Sam Stone gave her out of her purse. She fixes an egg salad sandwich and sits reading at the kitchen table. After a while, she heads upstairs to visit a website recommended in the pamphlet. For the third time in two days, she has to shoo Rachel away from George.

"Not now, Nana! I'm talking to Roge."

"But you have your own computer."

"Not like George. George is da double bomb." Rachel's fingers flash across the keyboard.

"The what?"

"Double bomb. You know, twice as nice."

As if by magic, George has replaced the HD-TV, Nana's KitchenAid stove, Jane's Pilates machine, and Rachel's iPod as the centerpiece of the Martin household. Molly the dog sleeps on a rug under the desk. Nana thinks George's screen glows brighter when people are in the room.

"Help me call up this website. I guess I need stronger glasses. I can't read all these dang backslashes and underscores. After 'www dot' it's what?"

"Dot whatever!"

Rachel is a sixteen-year-old with a rebellious streak. Growing up in a houseful of women, indulged by her mother, ignored by her father, she constantly demands attention and approval.

In those years, "reality" shows littered the TV networks, every one of them promising fame and fortune without the bother of education, discipline, or hard work. Millions bought into the fable that spread across the country like a drug.

Rachel is not happy being booted off the computer.

"You're not being polite," Nana says.

"Can't you wait until I'm finished?"

"Please lower your voice. Your mom may let you get away with being rude, but I'm not too old to paddle your bu ... bottom!"

"Yes, you are! And that would be child abuse!"

The two begin to giggle. A moment later, Rachel is back hanging on Nana's shoulder, trying to braid her hair into cornrows.

"Five more minutes?" she wheedles.

"Don't you have homework? I've got research to do."

Rachel shrugs and walks out of the room. Instead of studying for tomorrow's Spanish test, she reads *People* and *US* on her bed.

Nana rechecks the pamphlet, begins to type. Molly barks as a shadow, maybe a cloud, passes outside the window, plunging the room into gloom. Nana's fingers tremble on the keys. Without intending to, she hits the BACK button on the screen.

A line of text appears on George's monitor. *"Warning!"*

"Warning?" Nana hits ENTER.

A website pops open. Hip-hop music blares. Lots of gyrating teen flesh parades across the screen accompanied by moans and groans.

"Goodness!"

Rachel picks this moment to come back into the room.

Nana jumps as if scalded "I must have—"

"What do you think you're doing?"

Rachel's hands race across the keyboard. The images disappear. She turns and runs out of the room.

"I don't know what I did." Nana says. "What was that garbage?"

The girl slams her bedroom door behind her. Nana closes the laptop and pulls the plug.

"I have not been shut down prop—" squawks George.

Nana marches George, wires dangling, to her bedroom and shoves him in a drawer. She knocks on Rachel's door.

"Go away!"

She dials the phone and lambastes her Internet provider for promoting indecency, endangering vulnerable children, spreading immorality.

"Don't you have anything to say?"

Beep! The machine cuts her off. She's so wound up she suffers a dizzy spell. She sits on her bed, waiting for the lightheadedness to pass. Minutes go by, and her panic slowly seeps away, replaced by a feeling of helplessness and frustration.

Chapter 17

Walter's Café. Jane and Shelby are sipping wine at the bar waiting for a table. Jane is enthralled by a gossipy story Shelby tells about a prima ballerina who attended the Giulia School. Jane shrieks—too loudly, she thinks—at the punchline.

The conversation drifts in and out of the deafening music. Shelby is older than Jane first thought. Jane decides her legs are just as shapely as Shelby's, though she'd never wear a mini-skirt *that* short. Shelby has no children.

"I was all alone and struggling when Gerro showed up. He had some unusual friends who opened some doors for me. It was a blast while it lasted."

"What happened?"

"It gets old. There are a lot of negative ... *influences* out there. It's easy to get caught up. That's why I say you mom types don't realize how good you have it."

"Really?"

"Trust me. By the way, I told Gerro about Happy Kids. He's worked with kids a bunch. Did you know he's also a great photographer?"

"Wow, a real Renaissance man."

"You should see his photos. Absolute museum quality."

"Gerro. What an unusual name. He's got to be from somewhere else?"

"Like everywhere."

"I've been here my entire life," Jane says softly. "I'm the one who said, 'After college, I'm out of here.' Well, my friends left, and I'm here."

"What's keeping you? I mean, beside your kids?"

"I don't know. You believe in destiny?"

A flicker of something—sadness ... loss ... regret—crosses Shelby's pretty face. "I believe we all can choose," she finally says. "Make enough wrong choices, and you get to a point, well, it becomes your destiny."

"I don't look at it that way," Jane says. "I'm a romantic. I believe you can escape your fate."

"How so?"

"Through a great act of courage or faith." Jane doesn't know where those words came from. They just kind of, slipped out.

"You mean spiritual faith?"

"No, I guess I mean through love. I don't know. Maybe faith. I'm not sure." Sensing Shelby is uncomfortable, Jane changes the subject. "Gerro is welcome to drop by. I mean it. Most days, if I talk to a grown-up it's about leaky diapers."

"Poo. That's no fun."

"No, it's not. I tell you some of these kids—I'm talking about toddlers in seventy-five-dollar overalls—are starved for attention. I try to nurture them."

"I should think that's the parents' job?"

"They're too busy *parenting!*" says Jane. "Setting rules and boundaries. Worrying all the time. I'd like to shout, 'For God's sake, relax! Let go. Live a little!'"

"Relax? That's the answer?"

"Absolutely. Take my daughters. I trust them. They trust me. Trust is love."

"I see." Shelby clinks glasses with Jane. "Trust is love."

"You've got me going now," says Jane. "New Hope is this cocoon: Safe. Secure. Suffocating. Sterile. My butterflies are ready to spread their wings. Nana—wait till you meet my mom—thinks I'm out there in the ozone. Trust? Not Nana. Suspicion! She's a hawk."

A hostess arrives and shows them to their table. Both women draw appreciative glances from the men at the bar. The conversation, like the wine, continues to flow over dinner.

"I swear," Jane says, "some days, I wish the outside world would rush in and turn this town upside down."

"Careful. You may get what you wish for."

"Are you from a small town too?"

"Yup. Gilmer, Texas—near Tyler. You've never heard of it."

"How did you escape?"

"'Escape' is a funny word. Gerro is seductive. He's got this wounded quality. Don't ask me why, but I've always been drawn to that in a man. Usually, I'm the one who winds up wounded."

"Wow. I think I know what you're saying. Sarah and Rachel helped me through my divorce. I was really wounded. Now, it's my turn to do something for them. I want 'em to have things I didn't have. They're good kids, and I'm a good mother. I make sacrifices. I'm the first one at the soccer game, the first to volunteer to drive the cheerleading squad to away games." Jane sighs. "It's all great. It's just that, well, for one thing, I never date anymore." She catches herself. "Ah Jeez, listen to me."

Shelby has caught the eye of two guys sitting across the room. One of them toasts her.

"Never too late," Shelby says. "You just said we could change our fate through an act of courage. Isn't that what you said?"

Shelby is smiling, but Jane senses she's not joking.

"I'm not that brave at this actual moment," Jane says.

"I've never been," says Shelby. "More's the pity." She grows playful again. "Hey, I'm sure that cool dude in the blue sweater wants to buy you a drink."

Jane's hand rises to brush back a stray strand of hair. "Really?"

"Really."

"You think he's cool?"

Shelby looks at the guy, who is now posing like a cheesy fashion model. "Not really."

"I think it's time I go home."

"It's still early."

Chapter 18

The weather has grown chilly so I've asked Mrs. Brown to fix me a hot toddy, a small one. I'm going to sit, rug in my lap, by the crackling fire and push the weight of my burden from my heart.

Why do I believe New Hope was chosen? If it's true that no sparrow falls without His notice, is it so surprising that good and evil would clash in a rustic village a few miles from an interstate?

New Hope was always a special place, a community where love of God and one's neighbor remained strong.

In my lifetime, veterans returning from World War II became the teachers and preachers, civil servants and shopkeepers who keep a community strong. We started families and renewed our commitment, not in words but deeds. Perhaps it was the horror of that war that turned our gaze to the Lord. We struggled, not always successfully, to keep charity, decency, fairness, and equality alive in our hearts, rather than platitudes on dusty pages, the chaff of lifeless sermons. We promised to pass those virtues on to the next generations.

This revival, in which I played a small part, transformed New Hope into what President Ronald Reagan described in his farewell address as a "shining city upon a hill."

But with blessings come trials and tribulation. Darkness follows the Light as surely as night succeeds morning.

Inevitably, we drew the attention of the Pale Man.

Chapter 19

Halloween. Crumpled sheets of paper are scattered on the floor as Joe Adams tries to find the right words. He wants it all down on paper so there will be no doubt, no confusion about the secret he's kept, but his mind is whirling.

At nine P.M. he gives up, gathers his papers and rearranges his desk. He trudges down the school's stone steps—the "Adams bounce" has definitely been replaced by a defeated shuffle. He walks past the shoe factory over to Main Street and heads for All Hallows.

Another futile day. Twice, he'd gone to Alice Watters's office hoping to unburden himself; twice, he'd failed. Now, in the quiet candlelit chapel, he will confide in the Lord.

He climbs the steps and stands before the oaken doors. He hesitates. He can hear the choir at practice, how sweet the sound, but not for him. Joe cannot bring himself to knock at the door.

I imagine him standing there in despair. Was I deaf to his cry? I was Joe's pastor and Joe's friend. Why did I not seek him out in his hour of need? Did not Jesus command Peter, "Tarry ye here, and watch with me"?

I listened to the choir while a good man stood outside.

Joe walks away. A horn blasts. A car full of bloody corpses and howling demons roars by.

"Drop dead, Adams!" a creature shrieks.

A holy day, a time to remember the souls of the departed, has become a mad carnival. Another ghost is haunting Adams. Steve's image, proud in his dress uniform, pierces his heart.

"Why did it have to be my boy?"

He's asked the question a thousand times. The answer that leaps into his mind is a schoolyard jibe—"Y is a crooked letter." Adams has no answers and knows no forgiveness.

He walks toward Paradise Alley, a tavern off Main Street; its neon sign draws him like a beacon. It's crowded with costumed revelers. Joe sits at the bar and orders whiskey from the horned red devil mixing drinks. The man on the next stool turns to him.

"What do you know? Playing hooky on a school night?" The man extends his hand. "Remember me? Roger DeWalt."

Adams nods, shame burning his cheeks.

DeWalt eyes Adams's whiskey, pushes some bills toward the bartender.

"You've come to take me up on my offer!" he says grinning. "Cheers!"

Adams reaches for his drink. He feels the eyes of the men at the bar on him.

DeWalt nods at a woman in a clingy cat suit. "Say hello to my new friend Shelby."

"Trick or treat?" Shelby giggles.

Adams looks down at the bar.

"Loosen up, it's Halloween!" DeWalt says. "What have you got to lose?"

He catches the devil's eye and points at Adams's empty glass. Adams looks away. The devil slides the whiskey in front of him.

Chapter 20

Dorrie drives Nana to her appointment in the City. Along the way, she brings Nana up-to-date on the swindler who made off with her retirement.

"... Today the detective told me there's always a chance. He said to keep my hopes up. But the guy could be anywhere, using another name, ten other names. How do you find somebody like that?"

"If Jack were here, he'd figure it out."

Dorrie looks at her. "Pardon?"

"Jack. He fixed things."

"Nana, he can't. Not anymore. Don't upset yourself."

"Jack." Nana feels tears welling.

"Honey, Jack is gone. You've got to take care of yourself. That's what you told me to do. I'm trying. Believe me, I know it's not easy."

"I'm sorry, Dorrie. Sometimes I ..."

Jack gone. So many years, and his loss still cuts Nana like a knife.

The sedan bumps onto the Causeway. Dorrie, not the greatest driver, narrowly misses a guy in a black van yakking on his cell phone. He blasts the horn. Nana turns. She's seen him before.

Chapter 21

The office is crowded with patients, many elderly, some frightened and confused. Nana takes a clipboard from the receptionist and fills out a form. She notices it contains as many questions about her finances as her health.

In the examining room, Nana sits stiffly while a nurse draws blood and attaches a series of electrodes to her chest. At a desk, a technician inputs data into a computer. Nana feels like a specimen, not a person. When the internist, a young woman, arrives, she answers Nana's questions in vague terms.

"I'm not afraid. Tell me what you think," says Nana. "We're talking about my health."

"Mrs. Martin, it's way too soon." She says she'll send a full report to Dr. Stone.

Outside, Nana breathes in the hustle of the City, its throbbing energy. She can appreciate Jane's hunger for new people and experiences, but she also senses the anonymous, lonely souls walking right by her.

Dorrie bumps up to the curb. Nana gets in.

"Go okay?" Dorrie asks.

"Routine. Results in a week."

"Routine sounds darn good to me."

"Routine means they ignore you until you're too sick to cure."

"No, it doesn't. It means they're going to do their very best to figure out if something's wrong. And there probably isn't anything wrong with you."

Dorrie misses the entrance ramp to the Causeway. She nearly sideswipes a tractor-trailer. Nana shrieks.

"Glad to see you still want to live!"

Chapter 22

Nana boots up George, puts on her glasses, and tries to log onto a medical website she's discovered. Instead, a window opens, displaying a log of Internet sites recently visited. There are dozens and dozens, but one is blinking, www.popularkidz.net.

The site has been visited half-a-dozen times in the last twenty-four hours. Curious, Nana checks her desk calendar. Popularkidz is the site Rachel got so upset about the night Nana pulled the plug on George. She logs on.

"Oh, gosh." She watches a jittery video of a girl no older than Rachel provocatively … She grabs her mouse and closes the site.

She walks down the hall to Rachel's room, knocks on the door. No answer, and the door is locked. She moves down the hall.

"Jane?" she whispers.

No answer. She walks back to the office, sits down, tries to focus. She waits for her pulse to slow.

She realizes this is one of those critical moments that can send a family spinning into chaos or turn a rebellious or naïve child into a runaway or worse. She's got to be very careful. Nana decides to take time and think things through.

After a while, she logs onto her medical website. A definition appears:

anemia: a deficiency of red blood cells frequently manifested by skin pallor, shortness of breath, and lethargy.

She stands up, examines her reflection in the mirror just as Rachel appears in the doorway.

"Are you done? I need to use George to do school stuff."

"I just knocked on your door."

"I was listening to my iPod. Didn't hear you."

"Where's your mother?"

"I don't know. Out, I guess."

"We need to talk," Nana blurts.

"Not again. Puleeze!"

"PULEEZE!" echoes George, capturing Rachel's whine perfectly. Startled, they both stare at the computer.

"Just the two of us," Nana says. "Like we used to."

"What did I do?"

"We can talk about it in the morning." Nana studies her granddaughter. She recognizes her own features etched on Rachel's pretty face. So smart, so insecure.

"No, tell me what I've done."

"Maybe it's what you haven't done."

Rachel taps her toe impatiently, a gesture Nana finds supremely annoying. She suppresses an old-fashioned urge to give the teen a good smack.

"Tomorrow. It's late. Go to bed," Nana says. "You can get up early and use George. Then we'll talk."

Nana waits until Rachel is out of the room, then Googles *elevated white blood cell count*.

Sam said the condition could be caused by a number of things. Nana didn't hear that part. She continues to surf the Web. George is slow and balky.

"What now?"

Nana fingers the REBOOT button and starts over. She finds what she's been looking for:

> leukemia: a cancer of the blood cells in which the bone marrow produces abnormal white blood cells. These cells, over time, crowd out the normal blood cells.

She prints the document, sticks it in a desk drawer under some papers. She turns out the light.

She doesn't know what to type or where on the seemingly infinite Internet she can find solace. She sits there in darkness before heading to her bedroom.

Much later, she hears Rachel's door squeak closed.

"After midnight," Nana frets to herself. "On a school night."

An hour later, sleepless, she gets up and walks into the office. George's screen is pulsing bright red. She stands staring as instant messages begin pinging one after another.

The notes are truncated, filled with acronyms and abbreviations—CU, BBL, and HTH. Later, Nana will discover the letters mean "See you," "Be back later," and "Hope this helps."

What's clear is that someone—"Roge"—is inviting Rachel to visit him in the "chat room." Nana stares at the screen. She pecks at the keyboard to "flame" (she learned the term in class) the interloper. Instead of the familiar surge of power, George flickers and dies like a car with a bum battery.

Chapter 23

I've studied the Church Fathers, and I've read extensively enough in the literature of world's great religions to understand faith as an unbreakable bond between man and the Creator, a soul-deep hunger that cannot be denied.

I've come across other common, even universal themes. Again and again, I've seen the notion of Evil upsetting the natural order of things. The Scriptures, for example, are filled with parables of rulers whose corruption is reflected in their kingdoms and whose lands are plagued by drought and pestilence. We all know the story of Jonah, whose shipmates tossed him overboard into the mouth of the whale when they became convinced his sins were bringing disaster upon their heads.

Both Sophocles and Shakespeare used the notion in their tragedies. Samuel Coleridge's "Rime of the Ancient Mariner" recounts a similar curse. When the evil is cast out, balance is restored and the land is healed.

Evil had come to our city, but the threat went far beyond New Hope. Our nation was at a critical moment. The things we cared most about—friends and families, children, our schools, our faith, values and traditions, and most of all, our resolve—were under assault. Some attacks were overt, others more subtle, a slow unraveling of the social fabric. Was it technology tugging at the threads or simply a reflection of the human condition?

Chapter 24

Jane hurries into Happy Kids, dumps bags filled with diapers, juice, and other supplies onto the kitchen table. She drops her handbag to grab a jelly donut, takes a guilty bite, then tosses the rest into the trash.

She walks past the nursery and classrooms into the play area, where she encounters Shelby in a form-fitting leotard, demonstrating yoga movement to a group of ogling dads while Amanda Porter, one of Shelby's charges, hops up and down on a plastic chair trying to mimic Shelby's gyrations. Other kids wander in and out of the room, their faces smeared with jelly and peanut butter.

Sure enough, Amanda falls and cuts her lip at the precise moment her mother comes through the door. Both begin shrieking.

"My baby!"

"She's okay! It's okay!" Jane scoops Amanda up and races to the nurse's station. Other arriving mothers shoot angry glances at Shelby, who stands there as the fathers melt away. Jane rushes around swooping up children and scattered toys, straightening up, daubing faces.

When the panic subsides and the children have departed, Jane encounters Shelby in the kitchen calmly drinking a diet soda. Jane tells her Amanda needed a butterfly stitch.

"Breaks my heart," Jane says.

"I told her twice to stay off the chair. I really tried ..." Shelby eyes the clock.

"Shell, stay another minute. You can't *tell* a kid to do something. It doesn't work that way. You've got to get down to their level. Explain how they could hurt themselves. How sad Mommy and Daddy would be."

Shelby's face is an unreadable mask.

"Lacey Porter is a friend," Jane says. "Some of these other women would have been on the phone to their attorneys. We lucked out."

"We?" Shelby plucks at her outfit. "Jane, maybe I'm not right for this volunteer thing, especially with kids this young. I'm not used to responsibility."

"Of course you are. You're a professional suddenly having to deal with little kids. I understand that. Hey, let's put it behind us. Thursday is Sarah's recital. Rachel will be there. I've told her all about you guys. Please come. You and Gerro both."

"Jane, what if I'm not the person you think I am?"

"You're a great person. I know it."

"Jane."

"Yeah?"

"I don't feel so great." Shelby slips out the door.

At closing time, Jane makes her rounds, checking doors and windows, inspecting sinks and toilets, turning down the thermostat and, for the hundredth time, losing her darn keys. She grabs a spare set from under the rubber tree.

Chapter 25

Popularkidz.net.

Nana stares aghast at screen after screen of "Tween-Queens" and older adolescents posing in short shorts, halters, and skimpy underwear, children desperate to look grown-up and sexy. Dorrie stands at her shoulder, sipping tea and squinting at the screen.

"Where are their parents?" Nana says. "What are they thinking?"

"Haven't you seen the music videos out there?" Dorrie asks.

Nana notices popularkidz.net is linked to dozens of other websites, many of which require passwords for admission.

"Look at this. It's secret."

"I'm afraid it's the way things are going," Dorrie says. "No matter what we think."

Nana takes a deep breath. "How can you say that? You're a teacher."

"I'm afraid I'm not up to doing much crusading at the moment."

"I need to tell Jane. Don't you agree?"

"Yeah, I do, Nana. I've got to go meet with my lawyer. Good luck with this."

"You too. Any word on the investigation?"

"Not a thing."

After supper, Rachel and Sarah head into the living room to watch *Escape*, their favorite reality show. Alone in the kitchen with Jane, Nana mentions Roge's instant messages and this "chat room" Rachel has been invited to visit. She keeps the popularkidz.net stuff to herself for now. Dorrie had it right. Things are going in an unusual direction. *Straight to Hell*, Nana thinks. Popularkidz describes itself as a *legitimate fashion venue for the under-21 generation*. Unbelievable.

"Chat room?" Jane says. "How clever!"

"Clever?"

"You know, catchy."

"What's so catchy?" Nana counters. "I'm concerned. I think we should drive over there. Make sure it's—"

"Hello! You're missing the point. Chat rooms aren't real. They exist in … in cyberspace."

"Cyberspace?"

"You know … virtual reality? Didn't get to that in class?"

"I don't understand. Why are you being snippy?"

"It's been a long day." Jane doesn't mention the episode with Shelby. All she needs now is Nana second-guessing her unconventional approach to screening volunteers ("A hug?"), not to mention another lecture on trust.

She's off to pitch a group of parents on the benefits of Happy Kids' preschool program. Romper-Rhymer's headmaster will be there. Jane has heard some news about the big day-care center. Apparently, they hadn't bothered to install a CDC-recommended filtration system for their heating and air-conditioning units. Airborne viruses are a huge problem in day-care operations. A simple thing like workers failing to wash their hands after changing diapers can trigger an epidemic. She's torn between an urge to spread the rumor and her genuine concern for the kids.

"Mom," Jane says, "can we talk about this later?"

"That's what you always say. When I mentioned this Roge, Rachel got huffy. Told me to mind my own business and walked out of the room. Rude, don't you think? This is our business, right?"

"Wrong. You're alienating her. Trust me, Roge is some seventeen-year-old with pimples trying to be cool. This is how kids meet. The Internet is like this, this big schoolyard, a place for people to make friends and interact. Didn't you and Daddy meet in a schoolyard?"

"Steve Branigan was picking on me. Jack was driving by, he saw what was happening, and, well, you know your father had a temper."

"How romantic," says Jane as she reaches for her coat.

"Right, that's the answer. Sarcasm."

"Mom, I wasn't."

"Where does Roge live? Who are his parents? What if he's older or … not what he appears to be?"

"Mom, Rachel's right. Take a chill pill."

"Rachel's right?"

"You're overreacting. Worry, worry, worry! Before you go off again, what did Dr. Stone tell you? I'm worried about *you*."

"He's waiting for the latest test results. Routine."

"Routine?" says Jane. "What's routine?"

"You. He said you're routinely late for your checkup."

"Oh, dear." Jane glances at her watch. "Listen, I hear what you're saying. It's just ... well, kids act older today. They know more stuff. Yes, about sex, too. You can't lock them away from the world. It's impossible, and it's wrong."

"Kids are kids," says Nana. "They're vulnerable."

"All right. I'll talk to her when I get home. Okay?"

"Okay. But there's something else."

"Mom, you're driving me crazy. Can we talk later? I'm late."

In the car, Jane shakes her head. "Chat room! Senile. Just what I need."

She takes a breath and begins her mantra. "It's not how much you spend. It's how much you care ... Happy Kids We Care ... Start Happy, Stay Happy. No, that's not right ... Smart Parents Choose Happy Kids. Let's go, Brain. I need a little help here."

At the house, Rachel and Sarah do the dishes. Nana serves butter pecan ice cream.

"Not too much," Rachel cautions. "I'm watching my figure."

"Me too!" echoes Sarah.

"You're a string bean!" Nana says with a laugh.

"Am not."

"Are too."

Nana loves these kids so much her heart could burst. They talk about homework and school. Rachel's got a big math test coming up. Sarah asks Rachel to help her load a new game. Rachel's "like too busy," so Nana tries, and the installation works. She's feeling a flush of pride when the dizziness hits her.

"Play with me," Sarah pleads.

"It's late, honey. I'm tired."

"Are you okay?"

"I'm fine."

"You don't look fine."

"I am, really. It's just a silly ice-cream headache."

"Oh. Hate those."

Nana sits for a few moments to clear her head. George has stopped working again. Lines of error messages dance across his screen.

"I guess I did something wrong after all," Nana says. "Let's wait for Mom."

"Okay."

Nana asks Sarah if she can put herself to bed.

"Certainly, but you'll owe me a story about when you were growing up."

A few minutes later, Sarah tiptoes back into the office and kisses Nana goodnight. "Don't let the bedbugs bite! Remember, you used to tell me that!"

"It's wasn't so long ago."

"Was, too!"

Chapter 26

Ten forty-five P.M. Nana hears Jane's key in the lock. She checks to make sure the girls are in their rooms and heads downstairs to the kitchen. She must talk to Jane. She finds her scooping spoonfuls of cherry-fudge-truffle ice cream into her mouth.

"Hi!" Jane says between gulps. "I'm ... um, starting my diet tomorrow. You look pale. Are you feeling okay?"

"Fine. Must be all the blood they've taken out of me. I've been thinking about what you said. You're right about some of it. You know, allowing kids freedom and responsibility. That could be good within limits. Other things, I'm not so sure about. For example, how is an instant message from a stranger different from an anonymous phone call? Those are dangerous. Right?"

"Right," says Jane, rinsing her spoon. "You don't understand. I said I'd talk to Rachel. Last week, you were telling me you didn't trust George. For cripe's sake, George is an appliance, like a toaster! Do you distrust our toaster?"

"It could start a fire. And I'm not talking about George at the moment. George is a whole other story."

"How do you mean?"

"Don't get me distracted talking about George." She pauses. "Okay, since you ask, and I may actually be getting senile ..."

"No comment."

"George has a ... personality. It's distinct—gruff, grumpy, and occasionally sweet."

"Let me guess who."

"You're right. Sometimes I am reminded of your father. You think a machine can pick up on our feelings and emotions? Somehow mimic them?"

"I think you really miss Daddy."

"I do."

The two embrace. Nana fights the rush of tears.

"Daddy would probably see George as a tool allowing him to

open a window to the world."

"So do I! You can look out and see many wonderful things, but strangers can look in. If you're not careful, they'll ... catch you undressing."

"George is watching you undress? Okay, that's too much. I've *got* to get some sleep."

"We didn't get to talk."

"We'll talk tomorrow. Please, Mom, I'm beat."

* * *

An hour later, Rachel pads down the hall, sits down at Nana's desk. George boots right up. A smile spreads across her face.

"Yes!"

She hears footsteps on the third-floor staircase.

"Rachel?" says Jane blearily. "Is that you?"

Rachel types "P911" ("Parents are in the room!"), switches off the light, and disappears into her bedroom.

Ping ... Ping ... Ping go the instant messages.

For the rest of the night, the house is silent save for faint murmurings, Jane tossing and turning in her sleep, and Nana, sleepless, saying her prayers.

Chapter 27

The Elite Diner is empty except for a man in one of the booths going through a stack of newspaper clippings. It's the dead time between lunch and dinner. Dom wipes the countertop as he stares at the guy's reflection in the mirror. He's been in half-a-dozen times, just sits there, nursing his coffee, reeking of cologne.

In the booth, Roger DeWalt finds what he's looking for and smiles.

"Hey, bud, I ran into this guy the other night ... Joseph Adams. Know him?"

"My name isn't Bud." Dom hesitates. Why start off on the wrong foot? "I'm Dom. Everybody knows Joe. Good man."

"Whatever you say, Dom. That's Italian, right?"

"What about it? You gonna make a spicy meatball joke?"

The man sips his coffee, goes through a few more clippings.

Dom notices the guy is perspiring heavily. "Hot as Hell in here," the man grins. "Stay out of the kitchen, right?"

"Right," Dom replies. "To me, it's comfortable."

DeWalt glances at a photo of the New Hope High School Cheerleading Squad on the wall, a big *Thank You For Your Support!* scrawled across the top. Rachel Martin is in the front row.

"Good man, bad man. Who really knows?"

"Joe's a *very* good man," says Dom. "Why, you saying different?"

"If I told you I was a good guy, you'd believe it?"

"I don't know. Until I found out different."

"Then it would be too late." DeWalt grins as if he's scored a point. "Didn't Adams's kid get killed in the war?"

Dom rubs at a speck on the counter. "His son."

"Twenty-one years old, it says here. Damn shame."

"Joe never talks about it. We respect his feelings."

Dom looks up from the counter. "What did you mean by 'Who really knows?' I've lived in this town my whole life. I know Joe Adams."

"Forget it. By the way, what's up with you and DJ?"

"DJ?" Dom looks uncertainly at DeWalt, as if maybe he's seen the guy around town or something. "You don't know nothing about DJ! What are you, some kind of wise-guy debt collector? I don't owe nobody nothing."

DeWalt smiles. "Never thought of it like that. Debt collector? Why not?"

He picks up another clipping, waves it.

"Looks like the shoe factory is down at the heels! Get it? All these layoffs can't be good for your diner, no way. The trick is to know when to pull the plug." DeWalt sips his coffee, makes a face. "Ugh! How many years *you* been killing yourself? How many eighteen-hour days? Lost count, haven't you? Know what? Nobody cares. Not one person cares."

Dom says nothing.

"Maybe I can show you a way out. I bet Andy Stevens would be willing to let you out of your lease."

"I don't do too bad," mumbles Dom. Unaccountably, he feels that maybe, yes, his life *has* been a failure. "The business is what I know."

"Your own son doesn't respect you. That's why he wants out."

"How do you know?" says Dom, his voice strangled. "You really know my DJ?"

"Kids today," DeWalt says, holding his hands palms up. He mimics Dom's New York accent. "They don't care about nothin' but themselves."

Any other guy would be on the sidewalk dusting off his pants or worse, but Dom is stricken by DeWalt's words, paralyzed, a mouse mesmerized by a snake.

Suddenly, the man's attention shifts to a greater cruelty. He stands up, dead eyes following Nana's brown Buick making its way down Main Street. Dorrie is driving, and Nana, Yellow Pages in her lap, checks storefronts for a nonexistent "chat room."

Unaccountably, DeWalt shrieks with laughter. Dom turns and walks into the back room.

Chapter 28

Nana is on the phone with Manny, her computer instructor. From what she describes, he suggests George has "probably been infected with ..."

"... A virus?" Nana has read about the threats.

"A worm."

"What?" Instinctively, Nana wipes her hands on her sleeves.

That afternoon, Manny drops by to run diagnostics on George. He's impressed, like a teen glimpsing his first Ferrari. The machine, lightning fast, outpaces his testing equipment. An hour later, he's "dewormed" the laptop, though he can't find the renegade software.

Nana has the odd sensation the computer resisted, as if Manny were confronting a sentient force rather than some corrupt lines of code.

Manny finds configurations and programs, "black boxes," that he has never seen or read about. He decides George must be some hot-rod model being built overseas. He installs a tracking program designed to allow parents to monitor their children's Internet activity. Nana wants to present Jane with proof that Rachel's online behavior is risky, maybe even dangerous.

The red glow is gone, replaced by a bright field of flowers.

"That should do it." Manny twirls a Phillips screwdriver. "If you don't mind, I'll take a peek inside."

"You sound like my doctor. George isn't just an ordinary computer. He's ..."

"*He's?* Go on."

"Special."

* * *

George was not ordinary. You wouldn't believe that now, to look at the battered antique on my desk, its keyboard minus the letters F and L like a smile with missing teeth.

Over the years, I've thought long and hard over a question. *Is the appearance of a dramatic new technology any less marvelous than the parting of the Red Sea or the other miracles of the distant past?* Isn't the Greek myth of Prometheus, the titan who risked the wrath of Zeus by giving fire to man, really a story about technology? Why does the unmanifest become manifest?

Religious scholars say these "disruptions" took place in an age of miracles. Who's to say that age has ended? I imagine today's technological miracles as a speeding up, not a disruption, of the flow of the history of man.

* * *

After Manny leaves, an odd thing happens. A new window opens on George's screen. A stallion, wild-eyed, nostrils flaring, bucks and rears; after a moment, he grows docile. A great peacefulness settles over Nana.

That night, Jane finds Nana asleep at the computer.

"Momma," she whispers. "Let's get to bed."

When Jane returns to the office, a newspaper story, *Soccer Coach Accused of Molesting Youthful Charges*, is displayed on George's screen. Curious, Jane sits down to read it. When she finishes, another story appears, and then another.

Later, she decides George was simply processing searches Nana had keyed in earlier in the evening.

Chapter 29

Nightfall. In my mind's eye, I see the Pale Man in the factory tower. Does the wind howl? Does he imagine nature in obedience to him? Does he exult in his power over the mortals below? I imagine a glimmering laptop near at hand, keystrokes scurrying across the keyboard like mice in the dark, final names being added—Mayor Doug Lanier, County Commission Chairperson Jean Wilcox, Commissioner John McDonagh, PTA President Mary Farmer, Representative Peter Bowles. A message sent.

On Main Street, a driving rain keeps all but the desperate off the streets. Joe Adams emerges from the mist and stops in front of All Hallows, drawn by the light streaming through the stained glass windows. He cannot go in.

Joe moves past other houses of worship. Volunteers are arranging flowers, polishing candlesticks, spreading altar cloths for Thanksgiving services. Choirs are practicing. He approaches, craving fellowship. Hesitating, he hears the hymns yet moves on.

Two blocks away, Roger DeWalt exits the Savings and Loan building. He slips the property manager's business card into his pocket. He's sporting a new look, cashmere coat and fashionable suit.

Both men are drawn to the tavern's pulsing lights.

When DeWalt enters, he slips onto the stool next to Joe. He orders two double bourbons, points to Adams. "Let's run a tab."

He reaches into his coat and retrieves a yellow flyer. He pushes it toward Adams.

"This town is dead. I'm headed upstate to the casino. There's a show I want to catch. Why don't you join me?"

Adams shrugs. "I can't."

"Come on, we can make it by midnight," DeWalt urges. "I'll drive."

The bartender slides the drink in front of Joe. DeWalt makes small talk with Adams and the bartender. He glances at the tavern door, senses a ghostly figure hovering outside. He shivers and begins to talk faster, the disjointed words pouring out of him.

"Lemme tell you a story. My partner and I, we had our own shop. I loved the business. Had a great wife, loving daughter, though I didn't see them as much as I should have."

He sips his whiskey, talks some more.

"... A few years back, we go after this big apparel account. We're way over our heads, but we put together a fantastic pitch— I'm real good at this stuff—killed the competition in the review. We beat three big New York firms and won a forty-million-dollar account. That's ten to twelve percent, easy, in fees. We were still celebrating when the call came in. The CEO had overruled his own director of marketing and the consultants. He decided we were too small to handle the business. Awarded it to one of the big guys. You believe that?"

DeWalt gulps his drink.

"Well, we'd gone way over budget. I hadn't been home in eight or ten weeks. Our other clients were feeling neglected. A couple of them fired us. The rest happened quickly. Couldn't meet the pay- roll, and we'd tapped funds set aside for media purchases on other accounts—not a good thing. Well, I started gambling, you know, to recoup the money. I've always been a risk taker. It doesn't make sense unless you've been there. It's like a drug. I did okay then lost big ... our house. I couldn't talk to anyone, couldn't ask for help. That was the end of the agency.

"At that point, I'd hurt everyone who'd ever cared about me. My wife moved back to Arizona and took Kammy with her. Said she didn't want me around her! The kid has juvenile diabetes. I don't even know if she's gonna make it."

Adams stares at DeWalt who's tap, tapping the casino flyer on the bar with his finger.

"... I remember this one night. I needed to get away. Some place where nobody knew my name. Nobody cared that my kid was dying, that I was wasting all this talent. So I start drinking, and I drink. The rest is blurry. I stagger out of this place around dawn, and the troopers are waiting. Here I come, another drunk with a load of whiskey and guilt in his gut. They bust me—fingerprints, mug shot, sixty days in the tank with the losers, the whole enchilada. It changes you."

Adams has begun to tremble. DeWalt's words come to him in a jumble.

"That's why I can't work for the big firms anymore. Believe me, I'm not a great husband, not a great parent, but I feel things. I still need things. I still get hungry. I get lonely. When this offer from Digital Harvest comes along, I'm desperate. The boss doesn't ask any questions, and I don't say a thing. I jumped."

Adams hears something else: "And Mr. High School Principal is terrified his problem will filter down to the school board or the local newspaper."

The bartender pushes another whiskey at Joe.

"What?" Joe stammers.

"I said I jumped."

Adams hears: "Never eased up, did you? He was never good enough. Couldn't live up to your standards."

"No," Adams moans. His hands close around the letter in his pocket. "No!"

"I know I owe a debt," DeWalt slurs. "It's coming due. I'm going to take whatever I can. Now, while I can." DeWalt clinks glasses sloppily with Adams. "Come with me. Let's enjoy it while we can."

"No!" Joe throws some bills on the bar and rushes out into the night.

In the alley, inhuman laughter shrieks. Or is it the howling wind?

Chapter 30

Sarah's dance recital is a smash. She's cast as Belle in a scene from *Beauty and the Beast* and draws waves of applause. Afterward, Jane lingers to chat with parents before heading over to Happy Kids for an appointment. Nana and Dorrie agree to take the girls for pizza.

On the way, a van pulls alongside, blasts its horn and roars ahead.

"Crazy kids," Dorrie mumbles and slows another ten miles per hour.

Half an hour later, across town, Jane is pulling up to Happy Kids when she spots Shelby climbing into the driver's seat of a black van.

"Shell! We missed you. Sarah was fabulous!"

Shelby stiffens. "I ... I wanted to come."

Jane walks up to the van, hiding her disappointment and, typically, assuming the best. "It's okay. Actually, I've got some parents coming by in a little while. Maybe you can ..."

"I can't. Really."

The passenger window glides down. Jane glimpses a face, anonymous under a slouch hat. "Is that ... Gerro?"

A second later, a camera flashes, and Jane, blinded, stumbles backward.

"Hey!"

The van accelerates away.

Jane notices the day-care center's double doors are ajar and her lost set of keys is in the lock.

Inside, books and toys are scattered everywhere. Stunned, she walks down the hall to her office. Her computer is gone!

"Shelby! Why?"

At that moment, a silver SUV is parking out front. The driver honks the horn. It's the parents who are expecting a tour of the center. Jane, fighting tears, rushes outside, pulling the doors closed behind her.

"Mrs. Anthony, I'm so sorry," she blurts as the passenger door opens. "We'll have to do this another time. The ... pipes burst. It's a mess in there."

She stands there, helpless.

"These old buildings," the woman finally says. "You never know what's going to happen next. Why don't we call you tomorrow? We've done our research, and Happy Kids is at the top of our list."

"Thank you so much." Jane bites her lip to keep it from trembling.

The woman turns to her husband. "Hey, let's go grab dinner. The sitter is good for another two hours."

The SUV glides away.

"Please do," Jane calls after them.

Inside, part of Jane's brain registers that her stereo and TV are also gone. The rest of her is numb. "I would have given you the stuff!" she cries out to the empty street.

She begins to sob. When the police arrive, Jane has nothing, not a shred of solid information to give them. Shelby's address will turn out to be false, as will her story about the prestigious Giulia School.

"I trusted her," Jane tells the policeman taking the report. "I felt we were kind of like sisters."

The cop looks up from his scribbling. "How did you get to know her?"

Chapter 31

Later that night, Nana and Jane are in the kitchen. The initial shock of the burglary is now a throbbing pain.

"She could have hurt the children. What was I thinking?"

"She didn't. Thank God."

"I felt Shelby and I connected at this really deep level."

"You wanted to like her. She was different. A rebel."

"Right. Sophisticated and free."

"A liar and a thief. We're fortunate."

"Mom, thanks for saying 'we,'" Jane sniffles. "You know I'd be lost without you?"

"I think you just put your finger on the problem."

Jane hugs Nana. "Mom, I need to be more like you."

"What did the man look like?" Nana asks. "This fellow sat next to me in town a while back. I think his name was Walt or Walter, can't remember, but he gave me the willies."

"It was dark. His face was hidden by his hat. I couldn't see. "

Nana feels a stab of unease. "They sure went to a lot of effort to steal a computer and an old stereo," she says. "Don't you think?"

"Astral dance!" Jane says. "What a bunch of bull. What did I see in her?"

"A fantasy of yourself?"

Silence.

Nana pauses. "Did you hear what I just said?"

"You think I'm like Shelby? That's so mean."

"No. I'm wondering why Happy Kids? Why New Hope?"

"This was a random incident. I made it easy for them. Let's not complicate things with conspiracy theories."

Jane prefers to go on about friendship and betrayal. Nana knows what's coming next, a diatribe against Jane's ex-husband. She cuts her off. "Did you learn anything?"

"Keep track of my keys. I'm so disorganized, I don't even know where the insurance policy is."

"Keys? You let her in?"

"I did, didn't I? Maybe I should just shut Happy Kids down and do real estate. Andy Stevens said he'd hire me anytime."

"Yeah, that would solve everything." Nana takes a deep breath.

She can feel the dizziness coming. It's as if part of her brain is pulling loose from the back of her skull.

"Parents trust you. You've earned their trust. You do well with children."

"I like to think I'm childlike," says Jane, sniffling again.

Nana bites her tongue. A moment passes.

"Mom, tell me what I need to do."

"Shelve astral dance and yoga and focus on the basics. Can Happy Kids be cleaner, more nurturing, safer, or smarter?"

"Smarter? I opened my doors to a con artist. How smart is that?"

"Today, not very smart. The world has changed. People are often not what they seem or claim to be. When you were growing up it was different. Everyone knew everyone else. They knew who you were, where you were, and whom you played with. Everyone—your grandparents, aunts, uncles, Dorrie, the neighbors, Edna the crossing guard, Sister Malachy—kept an eye on you."

"No wonder I felt trapped."

"You felt loved. They were guardian angels."

"They must have left town."

"They've taken other forms. Times have changed, and the way we protect those we love must change. Have you heard about this electronic doohickey you stick on a kid's jacket? Allows you to follow exactly where he or she is, using your computer?"

"I read something about that in a women's magazine," says Jane. "There was some speculation that a few jealous individuals might try to use the devices to track spouses or partners."

"I hope not. There's a big difference between respecting privacy and making sure children are safe. I learned to trust people but only when they earned my trust. I agree, though, most people are genuine and basically want to do what's right."

"Now you sound like me."

"Most is not all. And it's definitely not strangers."

Chapter 32

The following morning Nana stares at George's screen, examining the tracking program Manny installed. Sure enough, Rachel has visited the Popularkidz website a dozen more times. She's been to some of the sleazy, password-protected ones too. Darn that girl!

Jane walks in, holding two steaming cups of tea.

"I've been thinking about last night," she says, handing a cup to Nana. "In fact, I didn't sleep much at all. Imagine, Mike Jones living around the corner. Sarah plays soccer with April."

"Sarah's fine. Dorrie spoke with her. You know, she still does volunteer youth counseling for the county."

"The idea of a criminal living right under our noses creeps me out."

"Happens more often than you'd think." Nana looks at Jane for a response, then sips her tea. "Dorrie told me Mike Jones's wife and kids have left town. They're staying with relatives. Sad, how the sins of the parents are often visited upon the children."

"April is a sweet girl. She was at Happy Kids for a while." Jane stares into her cup as if reading tea leaves, seemingly lost in thought.

"Remember my little lecture about guardian angels?" Nana prods.

"Guardian angels?"

"Yes. I said friends and neighbors used to keep a watchful eye. There are new ways to keep kids safe. Things you should think about."

"You mean that stick-on computer chip?"

"Lots of things. Background screening of employees, for example. You need to do things to convince parents that Happy Kids is a safe and nurturing environment and, well, that safe kids are happy kids."

"Convincing costs money. That's marketing and advertising. Big dollars. We can't afford that."

"More than advertising. Real steps."

Jane puts the empty cup on the desk.

"Romper-Rhymer had problems with kids getting sick," she says. "The state DHS inspectors came in and cited them. They've spent a fortune upgrading their systems. Now they're running TV ads about their 'pure environment' and offering sign-up discounts to recoup the business they lost. How am I going to match that?"

"Isn't Happy Kids' health record perfect?"

"Pretty near. Sam Stone keeps us on the ball. Hmmm." Jane pulls her chair closer. "You know, you said something interesting."

"When?"

"A moment ago."

"What? 'Your health record is perfect'?"

"No. Just before that."

"Umm. Safe kids ... are happy kids?"

"You got it backwards. 'Happy Kids Are Safe Kids.' That's it!"

"What's it?"

Jane jumps up and paints a sign in the air. "HAPPY KIDS ARE SAFE KIDS. It's great! Happy and safe! I'll show those Romper guys a thing or two. This is fabulous advertising. I've got a little money set aside."

"Advertising? I never said a thing about advertising."

"Yes, you did!"

Jane plants a kiss on Nana's cheek. In a flash, Jane is out the door and down the hall. "Wake up, you guys!" she shouts.

Jane knocks on bedroom doors and rattles doorknobs. It's Saturday. The girls have practice and lessons, dentist and haircut appointments.

Once again, there's no time to discuss Rachel's Internet wanderings. Advertising!

Nana shakes her head in frustration.

Chapter 33

Saturday night. Jane and Nana watch a film about a million-aire who falls in love with the spunky maid who cleans his hotel room. The rags-to-riches nonsense energizes Jane, who's usually nodding at ten P.M.

"Mom, before you turn in, help me set up George's design program. I've got some ideas I want to play with."

"Type 'design backslash C-A-D.' Manny showed me that."

"Showed you what?"

"Design backslash C-A-D. Don't worry. It seems George responds to the correct command regardless of what you type. How is that possible?"

"Probably a software thing. Google will automatically correct inaccurate queries. Let's not pretend a bunch of wires and chips can read our minds. And you're worried about me?"

"Still seems odd. I don't know, maybe I am getting senile."

Jane giggles at Nana's discomfort. It's as if the concerns of the past days have been swept aside. Sure enough, the design program pops right up. Jane sketches out some possible ads, fools around with taglines, then decides to check her e-mail. She's sorting through the usual junk mail when she spots a message: *Joe Adams, a Wolve in Sheep's Clothing!*

"Learn to spell, idiot!" she snorts. "Then get a life."

She opens it. A hundred names are on the address lines. Jane knows many of them. She spots Rachel's and some other students' names. She reads the message, then skims the official-looking documents attached to it. Joe Adams has been charged with *Driving Under the Influence—Alcohol, Reckless Driving, Striking Unattended Vehicle.*

"No way!"

She goes through the documents again. This time carefully. *Convicted: DUI. Reckless Driving reduced to Unsafe Operation of a Motor Vehicle. Five years probation and a five-thousand-dollar fine. License revocation: three years.*

"My goodness!"
Jane quickly forwards the e-mail to a dozen friends.

Chapter 34

The phone rings. Rachel dives for it, hoping it's Jamie. The quarterback drove her home from school last week. On Saturday, they had cheeseburgers at the Elite and like, really got along!

Only it's not Jamie. It's Roge. He's coming to New Hope to interview prospects for a summer scholarship program offered by Stars and Struts, "the world-famous cheerleading camp." Rachel is on the list.

"Mom! Mom!" she shrieks. "You're not going to believe it!"

She runs out of her bedroom and turns a somersault in the hallway, all thoughts of Jamie tumbling out of her head.

"Believe what, honey?"

In the office, Jane has the sinking feeling Rachel is shouting about Joe Adams. She kicks herself for forwarding that terrible e-mail.

"I could like win a scholarship to this famous cheerleading camp!" Rachel says. "It's called Stars and Struts. Get it?"

She grabs a pointer from the desk and begins to twirl.

"Wow, if I work really, really hard, I could make majorette! I'd really stand out!"

"Great." Jane is relieved. "Stars and Struts. Cool name. What happens next?"

"This really neat recruiter is like, coming to town in a few weeks to audition the finalists—me, Snotty Rice—hate her—and some other girls. It's the most important thing that ever happened! Roge says colleges give scholarships for cheerleading!"

"Really?" Jane leans forward. "Did you say 'Roge'?"

"Duh! He's the recruiter. Mom! You're not listening!"

"Oh, I'm listening. Great news! Won't Nana be surprised?"

Chapter 35

The next afternoon Rachel comes through the front door beaming. At school, some of the kids—Rachel knows they're jealous—made jokes about Stars and Struts ("the place for sluts!"). Not Jamie. He was happy for her. He told her he knew she'd do a great job. That really meant a lot. Now she'd try twice as hard to win.

"Hey, Mom! Guess what I found out!"

"What?"

"Jamie Kaufmann's grandfather and Nana went to school together. He had a crush on her till Grandpa showed up. Now it's Jamie and me! Is she upstairs?"

"At the doctor's, honey."

"Again? Is Nana okay?"

"I think so. Dr. Stone says her blood's a little thin."

"What's that mean?"

"You know, I don't know."

"Mom, isn't it your job to know?"

"It is, isn't it? I'd better start paying attention."

"Duh! Hey, you mind if I have dinner at Jamie's house? We're going to study together for a European history test."

Jane hesitates. "Okay, but call when you're ready to come home. No later than nine P.M. And no extracurricular activity."

"Mom!"

Mother and daughter giggle.

At six P.M., Nana arrives home. She excuses herself and heads to her room. Jane watches her slowly ascend the stairs. Rachel may be right to worry. Nana seems to have aged overnight.

After supper, Jane walks into the office carrying a sheaf of papers. Nana is staring at the computer. She turns to Jane.

"What's that? More medical insurance forms to fill out?"

"Afraid so." She takes a breath. "Mom, seriously, are you ... feeling okay?"

"Tired is all."

"Are you telling me the truth?"

"Yes."

"The whole truth? Don't make me worry." Jane hands Nana the forms.

"Have you seen this?" Nana taps the screen.

"What?"

Jane looks over her shoulder. "Oh, Principal Adams. I've seen it. My gosh, everybody has. Some reporters from WKNH in the City even showed up at the high school."

"Joe doesn't deserve this."

Chapter 36

The story was all over town. Joe Adams arrested and convicted for DUI! The school was in an uproar. To make things worse, some guy claiming he knew Joe was caught in the schoolyard spreading more terrible stories among the students.

I preached a sermon based on John 8:1-9: "He that is without sin among you, let him first cast a stone at her." It seemed to fall on deaf ears. After church, arguments raged.

"Who would do such a malicious thing?"

"The county commissioner is furious. He's up for reelection this year, and a scandal will hurt his chances."

"Adams is obviously guilty."

"Of what?"

"Read the e-mails!"

"Why would I?"

No one can stop the flow of information, particularly bad information. The Internet quickly took on a life of its own, overriding any attempt at logical discussion or honest assessment. Truth and falsehood were transformed into binary concepts, the yes or no, plus or minus. No explanation or nuance seemed to matter any more.

The significance invested in the written word, the historical record, verifiable facts, the eyewitness account, was being lost in the shifting sands of cyberspace. Every event, incident, interaction, or occasion was immediately open to interpretation, pulled and twisted like taffy until objective, verifiable truth no longer existed. It was lost in a blizzard of opinions and instantaneous analysis. If everyone is an expert, then no argument carries weight. No one is innocent until proven guilty. You're guilty until the man next to you stands accused. And the cycle begins all over again.

Riding home from church, Jane and Nana go round and round, trying to understand Adams's behavior.

"Joe is a good man," Nana says. "He's proved it time and again. That's what counts. Do you know he worked in Daddy's garage when he was a teenager? He put himself through school. Wouldn't take a penny from anyone unless he earned it. I want to hear his side. Sure, he's tough and unbending, but he had to be to survive. He's toughest on himself."

"Mom, he was pretty rough on Steve."

"He loved Steve. Don't you forget that."

"Did he? Did he ever show it?"

Nana looks Jane in the eye. "I got the same e-mail you did, only I deleted it. There are a lot of liars and frauds out there. Aren't there?"

"I guess so." Jane does not like hearing what she thinks is another dig about Shelby.

"Think about it," Nana continues. "This is a man's life and livelihood we're dissecting."

"You're right."

"Better right than fast."

"Did you just think of that?"

"Please, no more slogans."

Chapter 37

Jane spreads her research on the desk. This advertising idea really has her psyched. She picks up one news story after another.

"Unbelievable," she says to herself. "Page after page of people with criminal records working in schools and retirement homes. No one notices? Child molesters volunteering in scout troops, Sunday schools, sports camps, day-care centers! No one catches it? What's going on?"

She looks up. Nana is standing beside her.

"Look at these. Mike Jones is like the tip of an iceberg."

Nana squints at the headlines. "People are blind until something awful happens to them or someone they know."

"I think that's true."

"What about Happy Kids' employees?"

Jane taps George's keyboard. "Got it covered. Look here. Turnover in day-care centers is thirty percent a year. We've had the same people for ten years. I can talk about Ellie bringing in her nephew Ray all the way from Smyrna to be our cook. Two generations working in the same place. You never see that anymore."

"Jane, what do you really know about Ray? I'm sure he's fine, but wouldn't you want to be sure? I mean, after what happened?"

"Mom, Ellie is like family. I can't embarrass her like that."

Nana points to the pile of papers. "That's what everyone says."

Jane sits there a moment as if waiting for this unpleasant notion to go away. "Everyone I talk to says this could be the best advertising campaign ever!"

"Excuse me?" Nana says.

"I've decided to kick off a 'Happy Kids Are Safe Kids' ad campaign right away. Well, not a campaign. More like a couple of ads in the Sunday paper and the *Weekly Shopper*. I've e-mailed a couple of advertising agencies. One is new, right here in town. It's a great way to reach parents who are worried about everything ...

Show what a good job we do at Happy Kids. Hey, did I say something wrong?"

"You're still not listening."

"I'm listening," said Jane stubbornly. "Come on, Mom, don't start in."

"I'm just trying to make sure ..."

"Okay, since you want to talk about Happy Kids, we've got a very happy kid right here. Rachel! Remember Roge, however you say his name? Turns out he's a recruiter for this cheerleading camp. 'Stars and Stripes' ... 'Stars and Struts' ... something like that. Rachel is going to be competing for a college scholarship. She's so excited! You know how much she wants to be head cheerleader. It's a chance to shine!"

"That is good news. Did she get a letter?"

"Snail mail?"

"What?"

"Mother! E-mail! Roge got the girls' names and e-mail from Gloria Rice, Dottie's mom, and Rachel e-mailed him our phone number. He's talked to a bunch of the girls. See, all on the up-and-up. Just like I figured."

Jane reaches for Nana's hand. She's concerned about what she perceives as Nana's "mood swings."

"Mom, I know I messed up with Shelby. Everyone messes up. I need to move on. All I want is for Rachel and Sarah to have what you and Dad wanted for me. Not cars or fancy vacations. Opportunities! This cheerleading tryout could be nothing, or it could be the beginning of something wonderful. A scholarship. New places. New friends. New hopes! And then Rachel can thumb her nose to all those snooty girls with the cars and boutique outfits at school. I say 'Go for it, girl!'"

"With all the big high schools in the City, this man chooses New Hope High? Doesn't that seem a little odd to you?"

"Maybe Roge sees something special here. Why can't you accept that? You of all people, who's always saying New Hope is sooo great."

"Maybe he does see something." Nana points to the stories, glances at George blinking on the desk. "But we still need to know more."

"About what?"

"About everything."

Chapter 38

Jane bustles into the kitchen with Sarah. Nana has George on the kitchen table and is reading the newspaper on-line. She smiles at her granddaughter.

"Would George like coffee?" Jane says sweetly. "Or some toast?"

"You're funny."

"Wait for me by the car, honey. Don't forget your lunch. Pita pockets today."

"Why can't I buy lunch like the other kids?"

"You can. Just as soon as you do your chores and earn your allowance."

"That's child labor."

"Guilty as charged!" Jane turns back to Nana. "Rachel's got cheerleading practice. Can you pick her up?"

"Sure. I'll probably get Dorrie to drive. I'm a little shaky."

"I'd be shaky with *her* driving."

Jane checks her watch. "Don't wait on me for supper. Working late, I'll grab a sandwich." She takes a breath. "Did your tests come back? I want to know how they turned out? Don't just say 'routine' again."

"Should have the results this afternoon. My blood's a little thin."

Jane gulps a glass of liquid breakfast. "You keep saying that. Speaking of thin, have you lost weight? I've been trying to drop ten pounds for a year."

"Guess I needed to. They say you can't be too rich or too thin." Nana points to George. "You know, there's a way we can check out what Rachel's been up to."

"'Been up to?' What are you suggesting?"

"E-mail doesn't come out of nowhere. You can backtrack. Let me explain."

"Jeez Louise! Six months ago you thought a server was a guy who worked in a restaurant. I told you it's important to let teenagers find their way. We can't be spying on Rachel. Don't you read *any* modern parenting books?"

"Don't need to. I know the ropes. My mother taught me. Unlike you, I listened."

"Ropes? Maybe that's why I felt strangled! Mom, please allow Rachel her privacy. We can trust her. Don't go sneaking behind her back. She'd never forgive us." She puts the empty glass in the sink. "Trust is absolutely important, you know that."

"If we can't figure out who to trust," Nana blurts, "how can Rachel?"

Chapter 39

The phone rings. Nana stares at the caller ID screen—SAMUEL STONE MD—before answering. After a moment, Sam tells Nana her anemia can be symptomatic of "an iron deficiency, some forms of arthritis ... bone marrow disorders."

"Bone marrow? Give it to me straight, Sam."

"Excuse me?"

"I've been doing research. Leukemia."

"Whoa. You're way out of order. Did I tell you what I learned my first week in medical school? 'Anyone who does self-diagnosis has—'"

"'—a fool for a doctor.' Yes, Sam. At least a dozen times."

"Repetition doesn't make it any less true."

Now that I look back, it was also true that technology was changing the doctor-patient relationship dramatically. Along with millions of other patients, Nana was able to tap into a vast, user-friendly body of medical knowledge via the Internet and make informed decisions about her health care, though Sam was certainly right about the perils of self-diagnosis.

Certainly, we'd always need well-trained and caring medical specialists to manage serious illness, perform delicate procedures, and build trust and compassion into physician-patient interaction, but computers were increasingly sophisticated diagnostic tools. For example, the computers that mapped the human genome were now mapping the genes of cancer patients in an effort to isolate specific mutations that might have triggered the illness, a task far beyond the reach of any human diagnostician.

"What happens now?" asks Nana.

"What happens now is we move to the next step, a hematologist and some other specialists at the big hospital. They've got these new ..."

Silence.

"Are you okay?"

"You know, I've been thinking. When you get older, the word 'new' doesn't strike you as wonderful."

"When I was a kid, I thought science would create heaven on earth. No disease. No hunger. Flying cars. Peace on earth." He pauses. "Listen to me."

Nana hears him shuffle papers then take a breath.

"I can't rule out leukemia. I doubt it, but if that's the diagnosis we'll deal with it. There's different kinds, all nasty but often curable."

"I need time, Sam. I'm not ready."

"Whatever it is, it's going to be okay. That I can promise you."

"It's just ..."

"I'll have Rosie set up the appointments."

"Listen to me, Sam. I have things to do."

"I know that."

"You're not listening." She hangs up. Her hands move across George's keyboard, searching for something. After a minute, the words, "What seems to us as bitter trials are often blessings in disguise," appear on the screen.

She remembers she has to pick up Rachel. The phone rings. It's Dorrie.

"Come down. I'm running a little late."

"Where are you?"

"Outside. I'm on new my cell phone thingie. It works once you learn to ignore all the extra buttons. It takes pictures, too. Can you imagine?"

Silence.

"Nana?"

"I'm not getting into that little Bug of yours. We'll take the Buick." Nana hesitates. "Dorrie, I'm sorry."

"Is something wrong?"

"Your phone takes pictures? I'm afraid I'm not a pretty picture at the moment, Dorrie."

Chapter 40

Dom lives in an empty house crowded by memories.

DJ and his wife, Sally, live a few blocks away, but the clash over DJ's plans to grow the business has created this ... distance. Conservative by nature, Dom is worried about losing a livelihood handed down from his father. DJ, a newly minted MBA, sees the diner as a brand, a business to expand into "niche markets."

Dom doesn't know a niche from a ditch. He cares about family and relationships more than boosting his bottom line, though business has slowed lately. The diner is all he knows. He's hurt that his son, rather than learning from him, seems eager to ignore him. Both are hardheaded and emotional men. After their last quarrel, a nasty one, Dom stayed away. Since then, he's driven straight home after closing.

Over the years, Dom's customers—most of them anyway— have become a second family, right down to the obnoxious cousins and batty aunts. Dom loves people, and the regulars love the camaraderie and the homemade veal ravioli he serves on Thursdays. When Lucy passed after a long battle with lymphoma, the Elite was not a business but a life raft he clung to. How could he consider putting it at risk?

DJ has seemed to put the loss of his mother behind him. He has his own family to consider. His life is ahead of him. He's willing to take some risk. He's done his homework—time will prove his plan to expand into other markets right—but he doesn't have a clue about his father's feelings.

The house is a bleak reminder of Lucy and the life Dom once imagined would go on and on. He keeps his hurt hidden as best he can, volunteering in the community kitchen and delivering meals to the housebound. But so great was his love and so deep his loss, he has begun to drift away like one of the balloons at Nana's retirement party.

* * *

In those days, I made regular house calls just like Sam. I imagined myself a spiritual physician, out there taking the pulse of our community. Dom and Lucy's house was my favorite place, the company as abundant as the food.

I remember one particular visit a few months after Lucy passed. Dom was so distressed he said his soul yearned for release. I was taken aback; it took me a long time to find the words.

"God decides such things," I finally said. "God knows our suffering and our loss. Our faith tells us this cup will pass. Lucy will be waiting for you. Dom, your family needs you, and you need them."

I don't know if he heard me, if he *could* hear me at that moment.

Chapter 41

This time, Sam sends Nana to a physicians' group based at City Hospital for another procedure, a biopsy to look for an accumulation of abnormal blood cells. Nana grimaces as a doctor pushes a long needle into her hipbone and extracts a bone marrow sample.

How odd, she later tells me, that our destiny may reside in a few drops of blood. I comfort her with the thought that Christ's precious blood changed the course of human history. Science and faith are not in opposition.

Driving home with Dorrie, an unsettling proposition, it strikes Nana that she'd regret leaving things unfinished as much as she fears passing away. She'd bet most people feel that way.

"Dorrie."

"Yeah?"

"I'm sorry if I'm hard on you sometimes, or thoughtless. You're my best friend."

Dorrie reaches over to pat Nana's arm. "And you're mine."

"Careful!"

Dorrie exits the freeway, drives down Main Street heading to Nana's house. "Almost home."

Nana keeps the biopsy to herself.

That night, a great storm howls though New Hope, knocking out power lines all over the county. Nana, reading the Scriptures—George flickers but stays on-line—comes across a passage: *"But wilt thou know, O vain man, that faith without works is dead?"*

She wants to be faithful.

Chapter 42

Controversy swirled around Joe Adams. After all, New Hope was a small town. Even so, the depth of feeling that was stirred up shocked me.

Dom Palermo, of all people, sent Joe an e-mail, painstakingly typed and straight from the heart. He said he couldn't find the right words—none of us could—but he knew how much Joe Adams loved Steve. Dom and Joe had been Boy Scout leaders. Dom reminded Joe of the times they'd taken the boys camping on Mountain Lake—the fun, the good food, the sweet memories. Dom wrote:

> *I know what it is to lose the person you love most. To question almighty God. To never be able to say how much you loved them. Joe, you're my friend, the best friend DJ and the kids at the school ever had.*

Dom didn't realize that his message circulated all over town. Inadvertently, he'd used a broadcast e-mail format DJ had set up to advertise dinner specials at the diner.

A week passed; Dom had no response from Joe. By then, *he* needed to talk to someone, but he was either too embarrassed or too proud.

DJ was still meeting with this investor. They were already looking at properties with Andy Stevens. Is there a worse pain than your own flesh and blood abandoning you?

Dom had dropped by Joe's house a few times with take-out containers of food, dialed his number until his fingertips hurt, but either Adams was out or wouldn't answer. The holiday season was coming. Once joyful, it had become a nonstop loop of painful memories for Dom.

It happened on a Thursday evening. Dom locked the front doors after the last customer departed. He polished the slicing machine, scrubbed the grill, and waxed the floors with a circular polisher until they gleamed. He'd always liked the sound of the machine. It signaled the day was done.

At midnight, he carried the trash out to the dumpster. He locked the back door, stowed the computer with Nicky's pictures inside in his Dodge pickup.

Dom had nowhere to go. The diner he loved so much was driving away the son he loved so much. They couldn't communicate about the simplest things.

I believe the gap separating them was more than the tidal pull of father-son relationships. I imagine the Pale Man's hand at work. Roger DeWalt's appearance at the diner had plunged Dom into a depression so bottomless he could barely drag himself to work. He imagined despair settling all over New Hope like a toxic cloud. And so Dom ran.

The rain fell in sheets that night. On Main Street, Dom thought he glimpsed Joe Adams running as if pursued by demons. He braked and doubled back, tires skittering on the slick pavement. He circled the block.

If it had been Joe, Joe had vanished into the night.

Dom wasn't sure. Like most of us, he wasn't sure about a lot of things.

Chapter 43

When Nana made yet another visit to Sam Stone's office, she was stunned to find the Elite Diner shuttered. A FOR RENT. CONTACT ANDY STEVENS sign in the window. It hit all of us pretty hard.

The Elite closed? We sought explanations. We exchanged rumors. We were too busy to look beyond our own concerns, too familiar with Dom's gruff exterior to register the broken heart within, too comfortable with his generosity to extend him the kindness he deserved.

The worst of it was that Dom and Joe Adams were New Hope's rocks. We took them for granted even as the storms swirled and eroded their strength until there was so little left. Christ tells us our neighbor's pain is our pain.

And we let the cup pass.

Chapter 44

Crossing the town square, Dorrie runs into Bob and Erma Gabriel. She's just met with the district attorney. Not a word about the crook who'd ripped her off. He's gone, and they'll never find him.

"What's this about Principal Adams?" Bob asks. "Everyone at the club is talking about it."

"It's true," says Dorrie, "but not the whole truth."

"Can't be true," says Bob. "I know Joe. He kept an eye on our sons even after they'd started college."

"We need facts," says Erma. "All these rumors chasing each other. Bob, you play golf with the school board chairman. What's his name? Abby Christopher's husband?"

"Maynard. I'll see him tomorrow at the Chamber."

"Call him tonight. Joe lost his son, for gosh sakes. Of course he's vulnerable. Bob, I have a bad feeling."

On the other side of town, Nana's fingers glide along George's keyboard. She, too, has been e-mailing Joe Adams. She too, has a bad feeling. This time, George displays an error message: "*Mailer-Daemon Returned Mail: Permanent Fatal Errors.*"

What in the heck is a mailer demon? She sends an e-mail to Dom, asking if he's heard back from Joe. She mentions that she'd seen Nicky a few times at Happy Kids' after-school program. "He's getting so tall!"

Days pass without a word. Nana prints both men's e-mail addresses on letters that remind the community of the importance of reaching out to those who are vulnerable and hurting. She mails dozens of them to church members; many are seniors who ask their children and grandchildren for assistance. They, in turn, get involved in the outreach. Her good works establish new bonds where the generations were perhaps drifting apart.

Chapter 45

Dorrie watches as Nana surfs one medical website after another, researching the best doctors and the handful to avoid. Fascinated, she asks Nana to give her pointers on using the Internet. In an hour, she's surfing the Web, sending e-mail to her daughter and grandkids in California.

"This is amazing," Dorrie says.

"I knew you'd think so."

Dorrie starts to stand up. "Don't you want George back?"

"No, you go ahead. Enjoy yourself." Nana excuses herself and heads to her bedroom for a rest.

Twenty minutes later, Dorrie's shout brings her hurrying back down the hall.

"What's wrong?"

"Look at this! They caught the miserable son-of-a-gun who embezzled my money. He was in Chicago! Look, it's right here."

She taps George's screen. "'Philip Green arrested on multiple charges of wire fraud.' He's the guy! He was doing it again!"

Nana squints at the screen. She's blind without her glasses. She reaches into the desk drawer.

"It says the U.S. Attorney has ordered Green's assets frozen. That's my money!"

"Wait a minute. This happened weeks ago. Why were you looking at last month's *Chicago Tribune?*"

"Weeks ago? And our louse of a district attorney didn't notify me. He makes me so angry. What if I hadn't seen this?"

"Dorrie?"

"Yeah?" She's obviously distracted.

Nana stares at George and back at Dorrie. "Why were you looking at a Chicago newspaper?"

"I wasn't. It just sort of popped up on the screen."

"'Sort of'?"

Dorrie is staring at the story. "Darn, it doesn't say how much money they've recovered. I'm going over to the courthouse and have a talk with Mr. District Attorney right now. I believe he's got an election coming up."

"Dorrie, he couldn't have located this man. He was in Chicago."

Nana tries to remember if *she'd* programmed an on-line "financial scam" alert into the computer. For the life of her, she can't recall. She gives George a peculiar look. The flowered screensaver suddenly appears, covering George like a veil.

"Hmmm."

After Dorrie leaves, Nana comes across another odd coincidence, a story about a high school cheerleading coach dismissed for inappropriate activities. Her concern over Rachel and this contest comes roaring back. She runs searches on "Stars and Stripes," "Stars and Struts," and other variations, encountering a blizzard of pop-up ads, many of them vulgar or outright fraudulent. Either too much or nothing at all comes up on "Stars and Struts." She spells the words five different ways. She types in "cheerleader + Stars and Struts." Nothing.

She's still sitting there when Jane bursts in carrying an oversize manila portfolio. Jane opens it and slides out a poster that reads:

HAPPY KIDS ARE SAFE KIDS!
ENROLL YOUR CHILD IN NEW HOPE'S
PREMIER DAY-CARE FACILITY.
WE'RE PARENTS. IT'S OUR JOB TO CARE.

"What do you think?"

Nana stares at the poster and nods. "Exactly what I've been saying."

"I think we both came up with the concept," sniffs Jane.

"That's not what I mean."

"I'm telling you every responsible parent will go for this."

"Of course they will." Nana pulls her gaze away from George. "I'm talking about *our* girls. What if this camp is a scam like Dorrie's financial planner? Do you want Rachel to be hurt?" She taps the computer keys. "I've been checking. I can't find a single thing. What's Roge's last name?"

"I never asked. Did you? I'm worried about Happy Kids. I'm trying to stay in business. For gosh sakes, he's a salesman. Ten of them call me every day pitching something. Rachel knows what she's doing. I don't know a lot of people's last names."

"You should."

"Why, because of Shelby? That was a mistake. I learned my lesson. Let's move on."

Mother and daughter go back and forth in this endless argument. The discussion ends with nothing resolved. Nana still can't find a way to mention Rachel's late-night visits to popularkidz.net's chat room without looking like a sneak.

Chapter 46

While Nana sleeps and Jane sketches out ideas for her Happy Kids campaign on the dining room table, Roge instant messages sleepless, star-struck Rachel. It's confirmed. He'll be in New Hope before Christmas.

"I'll be at the Market Hotel. Only the finest for our candidates!"

Using the shorthand spellings and acronyms peculiar to young people and instant messages, he tells Rachel he'll be conducting the cheerleader interviews, but additionally he's handling a nationwide search for a talent agency.

"Competition is tough," he writes. "OBTW (Oh, by the way), I can tell you Betty Edwards is competing and Dottie Rice is going all out to win the scholarship."

"Dottie!" Rachel gasps. Her face, a mask of spite and frustration, stares at her from George's screen.

"I knew it!" she hisses. "Damn her!"

After a moment, she begins typing.

"OIC (Oh, I see). Roge, I think you should know that Dottie was suspended for a drinking incident last semester. And I've got better grades. You should also know ..."

Rachel feels a twinge of guilt but tells herself she's behaving no differently than contestants on the reality programs she watches. It's dog-eat-dog out there.

"... THX," the IM flashes back. "Understand your concern."

"Can't she be uh ... disqualified?" Rachel types, ashamed of herself.

George's screen wavers for an instant. Then another IM: "How badly do you want to win?"

"Do anything," Rachel types grimly.

"EG (Evil grin)! That's the commitment I'm looking for. Of course, I'll want additional material for the talent search, some high-fashion shots. You've seen my website. You have a portfolio, yes?"

Rachel cringes, thinking of her scrapbook of stupid pictures. "Not really."

"I'm handling the photography. Our wardrobe people can send along some outfits. Unless, of course, you've got something?"

Rachel imagines Snotty Dottie flaunting one of her hot outfits then thinks of her own embarrassingly adolescent wardrobe.

"Bring them!" she types, feeling oh-so-grown-up. "Size four."

"TTYL" (Talk to you later).

Chapter 47

When Sam Stone calls, Nana grabs the phone, not wanting to upset Jane or the girls.

"I didn't want to keep you waiting. For some reason, lab results always arrive on Friday afternoons." He clears his throat. Nana hears him shuffling papers. "Your biopsy was inconclusive. They're going to do it again in three weeks."

"Sam, you said this test was definitive."

"The only definite things are ... you know."

"I know. Sam, sometimes your plethora of homilies gets on my nerves. Aren't you going to tell me 'No news is good news'?"

"Actually, no news can be *pretty* good news." He hesitates. "Hey, do you and Jane want to have dinner with me and Rose tonight? We can talk some more in person. There's this new place on Main Street. Chez Something or other?"

"Thank you, but I've got stuff to do and Jane is, well, really busy. Let's do it another time." Nana wants to keep Jane out of any discussion about her health for now.

"Don't put off till tomorrow what you can do today."

"Sam!"

That night, Nana dreams she's wandering in New Hope Cemetery. She senses something stalking her. She jolts awake in a cold sweat, tosses and turns the rest of the night.

Morning. The sun shines, and the world seems a happy place. Jane and Sarah walk into the office to wave at Nana, who's feeling fuzzyheaded. They're off to a soccer game.

Sarah wears a hooded red warm-up suit. "Do you ever get off that computer?" she asks.

"Well, well, it's Miss Red Riding Hood!"

"Mom, Nana's making fun of my hair! I'm gonna get a complex."

"Are not."

"Am too."

Nana tries to hug Sarah, who steps back. So she opens a tin of cookies. Sarah quickly grabs two.

"You're too fast for me," Nana says with a laugh.

"You spoil this child rotten," says Jane.

"I'm hardly a child!" Sarah gobbles the cookies. "Are you coming to my game?" she asks, wiping crumbs on her sleeve. "Coach Dowling made me goalie."

"Honey, I'm worried I'll catch cold."

"Nana, you worry too much."

Nana reaches out and grabs her. "You should worry about the big bad wolf!"

"Help!" Sarah giggles despite herself. "Mom!"

"Stop treating her like an seven-year-old."

"Yeah, I'm eleven!" She runs out of the office, pounds down the stairs.

Jane reminds Nana to rouse Rachel, dead asleep, in time for New Hope High's playoff game at one P.M.

"Jane, wait one second. Let's be serious. I've been trying to talk to you for two weeks. First there was the break-in. Now you're on this advertising kick, so I guess I never will. I'm going to ask Alice Watters what she thinks about this cheerleading competition whether you like it or not. Her husband is a detective, you know."

"And for two weeks I've been telling you it's no big deal. What's the worst that could happen? They try to sell the kids something? Coach Watters is a grouch. She put *me* down when I was in her English class. Don't let her undermine Rachel."

Nana, who knows Watters very well from her book club, ignores her.

"Listen to this. I called the school to get some parents' e-mail addresses. The registrar said they don't give information out without permission."

"Gloria Rice gave them out! Everybody has everybody else's e-mail. Go ahead, be distrustful. How is anything going to happen in New Hope if we don't open our doors a crack?"

"I don't want anyone showing up at *my* door uninvited. Every time you think someone is ..."

"Mom, I know you're not feeling well, and I understand your concerns, but life is complicated. I can't reduce it to your simple rules. 'Do this. Don't do that.' 'This is bad. That's good.' Nothing is black and white. Guess where I got the inspiration for the Happy Kids ad campaign? That's right, from Shelby!"

Jane turns and walks out the door.

Chapter 48

Dorrie decides to buy a computer. She runs into Bob Gabriel at the computer store. The salesman, an electrical engineering student, has no idea what she's talking about when Dorrie describes Nana's "whiz-bang" computer that anticipates commands and seems to have its own personality. He says what she's describing doesn't yet exist.

"Yes it does! I've seen it. It's called a George."

Another salesman walks over. It's Nana's buddy Manny. "Mrs. Smith, where *did* Mrs. Martin get her computer?" he asks.

Bob clears his throat. "From me. Special-ordered it myself. I want one too."

Actually, Bob's secretary, Bernice, found Bob's memo buried under a pile of papers three months later. That particular order had never gone out.

"I've got this Apple on sale."

"Apple? We want a George."

Chapter 49

Phone calls and e-mails circulate among New Hope County's school-board members, its teachers, parents, and students, who'd been personally touched by Joseph Adams. The outpouring is so great it seems Joe will be lifted from the depths like a diver, lungs bursting, who makes his way to the surface and gulps life-giving air.

Not one message reaches Adams.

Instead, a letter arrives from an attorney tendering Joe's resignation, surprising Maynard Christopher and the board, who'd agreed, over the objections of their lawyers, to extend a vote of confidence.

News of Adams's departure—twisted and exaggerated by rumor—reaches faculty and PTA members. At an emergency meeting, they mistakenly attack the bureaucrats for abandoning the beleaguered principal. Other parents, mostly newcomers, insist Adams's dismissal is the right decision. The board selects Alice Watters, the no-nonsense English Department chair, as Joe's replacement.

The arguments are so bitter and divisive they remind Dorrie of a line from a Shakespeare play she'd taught at the high school for many years:

Confusion now hath made its masterpiece.

—Macbeth

Chapter 50

Joe Adams fell apart six months to the day after the chaplain and the captain who'd commanded Steve's U.S. Army Ranger company arrived in New Hope. One night, desperate to outrun his grief, he stumbled on a casino deep in the northern forest. Hours or days later—Adams couldn't remember—he staggered out into the pouring rain, heading for the parking lot. Ten minutes later, Joe's car swerved into an overlook and smashed into a stone guardrail. He was somehow unhurt, but when the state troopers arrived, they had to wrestle Joe *away* from the cliff and the boiling stream five hundred feet below.

He pleaded guilty to DUI, offered no explanation, and sought no mercy. The county judge decided to make an example of this renegade educator.

For two years, guilt over Steve's death had eaten at Joe's heart like acid. Now it was exacerbated by a toxic mix of shame and hypocrisy. One evening, when he could bear no more, Joe unlocked the white 1963 Mustang he and Steve had restored. It started right up, which made Joe weep a final time.

He drove the forty miles to Mountain Lake on roads slippery with ice. He parked in a small cove near the cabin Sam Stone had built on the lake's eastern shore. I believe it was there that the Pale Man revealed himself, a shadow among the trees.

The ground sparkled like tears. Stars glinted coldly on still water.

Ironically, Sam had prescribed a sleep medication to help Joe through his torment. Adams had endured the pain and ignored the pills. Now, he pulled the brown plastic bottle from his jacket, unscrewed it, and began methodically ingesting the pills between sips of water, ten ... fifteen ... twenty. He lost count. He fought the urge to gag, and later, as he began to slip into darkness, his hand jerked at the door handle as if trying to escape.

A week later, Sam, who'd driven up to do some soul-searching of his own, found the body. Sam carefully wrapped his friend in blankets he pulled from the cabin beds. He brought Joe Adams home.

A letter closes this terrible circle.

Joe never got it. A surgeon in a field hospital had found it in Steve's fatigue pocket. In the crush of combat he didn't forward it until much later, when it got lost in the army's endless bureaucracy. It finally arrived in New Hope days after Joe's death.

Today, it rests with Joe above his heart. I cannot bear to write the words, but it was a message of love that gave lie to all Joe's doubts and fears, all the guilt the Pale Man had sown.

Steve idolized his father. His fierce patriotism and devotion to duty had been learned at Joe's knee. Discipline had served him well, tempered, as it was, by love. Steve had left not out of anger but duty—and only to answer a deeper call. He knew it broke Joe's heart to see him go, but this was knowledge fathers and sons often keep to themselves.

"I want you to know how much I love you," Steve wrote. "All that I am has flowed from you."

Chapter 51

Christmas was approaching, an incandescent spark of hope in the midst of darkness, a signal that life, the tumultuous roller coaster of human existence, goes on.

Those eventful weeks would set the course I would follow in the decades ahead.

Sorrow and joy—man's earthly lot—unfolded in equal measure.

* * *

A few blocks from Joe Adams's house, Teresa Carson, Jane's high school friend, gets a call from Sam Stone. He tells her the lump on her breast is benign. She drives to All Hallows to offer prayers for the less fortunate, and for the rest of her life, she decorates our altar with flowers.

At New Hope County Hospital, Dorrie's niece, Leslie Roberts, gives birth to healthy twins, ending a decade-long battle with infertility. The boys, Joseph and Stephen, are baptized in the dawn of the New Year.

At New Hope Cemetery, David Donnelly—he played with Jack and me on New Hope's championship football squad—is laid to rest two hundred feet from Nana's family's plot.

At the high school playoffs, Jamie Kaufmann throws an effortless touchdown pass to a receiver streaking down the sidelines. The crowd roars. Jamie jogs to the sidelines as the cheerleaders rush onto the field. He executes an elaborate bow in front of Rachel, making her day.

At ballet class, Sarah executes a perfect fouetté and basks in her instructor's praise.

In the City, a new generation of parents stare at the readouts in the corners of their computer screens (the office clock has vanished) eager to be home with their families, wondering if the traffic on the Causeway will be jammed again.

Chapter 52

Sam Stone reviews a stack of lab reports he pulls off the office printer. He double-checks Louise Martin's paperwork. What was "inconclusive" now seems confirmed.

He logs onto New Hope Hospital's intranet, punches in a code, and clicks on PATHOLOGY. He types in Nana's identification number, shaking his head as the numbers crawl across the screen.

Nana's red blood cell count has dropped precipitously. A particular white blood cell critical in defending the body against disease is almost nonexistent. Stone has never seen a case develop this rapidly. The evidence points to acute lymphocytic leukemia (ALL), a fast-moving, fatal illness.

Sam shuts down the computer. He removes his reading glasses, tucks them carefully into his desk drawer. He checks his watch—it's late—and drives home. He'll wait until morning to deliver the news.

Nana is still asleep when the phone rings. Jane, flipping through a magazine at the kitchen table, glances at the caller ID and grabs the phone.

"Sam?"

"Mother around?"

"Sleeping. She's been really tired. Not herself."

Stone clears his throat, sending a tickle of panic through Jane. "You understand your mother recently gave me permission to discuss her case with you?"

"Sam!" Jane fights to stay calm. "Yes, I do."

He describes the lab results.

Jane listens for a moment then blurts, "Oh, God! Oh, dear Jesus!"

Sam allows Jane a moment to compose herself. "No one knows how this will turn out, but Nana's going to need your support. She's got a battle ahead of her."

He tries to answers Jane's questions, but she's not hearing him. Not really. She wants to know if Nana is going to die. It is a question everyone asks and no doctor can answer with certainty.

He'll stop by later to visit.

Jane cannot see the deeper truth—the endless, loving continuum of creation that gives lie to the Pale Man. A benevolent deity, Jesus Christ my Lord and Savior, extends each of us the promise of eternal life, a source of strength Nana and Jane must embrace.

I myself have cried out to God to take me home. I've outlived my wife, Anna, and both our beloved children. I've grown weak in body and spirit. But by His grace, my strength is renewed.

And by His grace, my tale continues.

Chapter 53

Nana takes the news calmly. She offers Sam coffee and pie. They discuss what lies ahead, likely a regimen of powerful anti-cancer drugs followed by ever more tests. Her life, once so expansive, will be lived in three-month cycles. When he departs, she retreats to her bedroom and sobs, afraid of pain, afraid of dying, afraid for Jane and Rachel and Sarah, the familiar torment.

I remember her at services that Sunday. She wore her best dress; her sweet soprano soared over us as we sang our hymns. Somehow, as it always does, word of her illness had begun to spread.

"I'm not doing well, Pastor," she said, "but I'm going to be fine."

"God is there for you." I could say no more.

She moved on, allowing others in the congregation to approach me. I noticed her uncertain step straighten, her head tilt upward, projecting strength to all. After a moment, I lost sight of her in the bright swirl of people gathered outside the church.

* * *

At noon, Nana steps off a bus and walks through the gates of New Hope Cemetery. Above her, silver contrails of airliners bisect the sky. In the distance, cars hum along the Causeway. Microwave towers sprout like weeds, reminders that New Hope is no longer a small town but part of a larger, interconnected world.

As Nana makes her way up a hill, a mist appears among the gravestones. A moment later, she senses something, a thing rancid and decayed, like the maggot-ridden meat she'd discovered when the basement freezer failed. Instinctively, she crosses herself.

She hears a sound like the beating of wings. Nana turns. On the next hill, a scarecrow stands in a garden of stone. She has the uncanny feeling a camera lens is probing her soul. The world begins to slow on its axis. She feels the first tickle of dizziness and darkness descending. She whispers a prayer.

Abruptly, the air churns as if buffeted by some unseen force. Nana hurries the remaining yards to the Martin family plot. She looks around. Stillness.

She kneels down, plucks stray leaves of grass from the grave. After a moment, she begins speaking.

"Jack."

Only the trees whisper in reply.

"Jack, I've had these tests. Sam says I'm sick. I'm very sick."

She dabs her eyes. "I remember what you said when you were ill. You said, 'If that's what God wants, we'll deal with it.' I don't think I can deal with it. I promised to take care of our family. I haven't. And now, there's ... there's ..."

She pauses, takes a breath.

"There's something else, something evil. I can feel it, Jack, the thing that ripped the heart out of Joe Adams. He's dead, and now Dom has disappeared, nobody knows where or why. Other things aren't right, not right at all. I worry about Jane and the girls. What if it's stalking them? I don't know what to do. I don't know how long ..."

Nana pauses, fighting tears. She unwraps a bouquet and arranges it on the grave.

She stands. She senses a shadow cross the grave. And then high above her, an airliner is silhouetted against the azure sky, a cross flashing in the sunlight.

In an instant, Nana's fears are cast away. She looks around. The shadows have vanished.

Chapter 54

In a hotel room overlooking Temptation Mall, the man known as Roger DeWalt stares at a trickle of Sunday shoppers. The unmistakable brass and thump of a marching band floats up to him. He stares, sees Rachel and Dottie strutting in front, ready to perform for the afternoon crowd.

His eyes pick out a younger child, a girl with fiery red hair walking alongside Rachel.

Sarah.

DeWalt imagines the evil lurking in the shadows, pressing him, compelling him until the need to hurt and ravage surges like a drug. It's easier for him that way. He tears his eyes away from the child and returns to his laptop.

In an instant, the names appear on his screen: JANE MARTIN. RACHEL MARTIN. SARAH MARTIN. There! Louise Martin. There was something about that meddling old woman, an unexpected strength or power he couldn't understand. Somehow he had to get past her, and then nothing would stand in his way. The thought strikes him: *I can get to her through her loved ones.* His smile is without humor.

In the old Victorian, George comes to life, startling Molly, asleep under the desk. Millions of bits of code race across his monitor, his processors accelerate. Programs, etched on his hard drives, begin running, flooding his memory, engaging him.

The stallion Nana glimpsed in the machine appears once more, bearing a knight arrayed in armor. The knight lowers his lance and charges.

In the hotel room, DeWalt's keyboard clatters. A few seconds more ...

A millisecond later, an electrical surge crackles through the machine. DeWalt's fingers register an unnatural heat. He pushes back violently from the desk; his chair overturns, dumping him on the floor.

In the office, George returns to "sleep" mode.

Time passes. I imagine the Pale Man, who is relentless, in his tower. Files embedded with hidden commands spread like toxins through the servers and data networks linking New Hope to the rest of the world. He shuts them down.

Chapter 55

When Jane tries to print the HAPPY KIDS ARE SAFE KIDS! ads she's been working on, George freezes up and won't reboot.

"Darn!"

She walks down the hall, listens for a moment at the bedroom door, then decides to let Nana rest. She goes downstairs to the kitchen, locates Manny's number on a pad, and flips open her cell phone, grabbing a cookie with one hand as she dials with the other.

Manny tells her that the Internet service providers serving New Hope are having problems.

"Weird. It's like the pipes are clogged. Some things get through, some don't."

"Pipes? I thought cyberspace was ..."

"No ... No. It's well ... you've heard that the Internet is a highway. Traffic can be flowing smoothly—think of the Causeway on a Sunday morning—but you're all stuck on an entrance ramp because of an accident or roadwork or something."

"Something? Like what?"

"Don't know. It's like this ... this electrical storm is sitting over us, messing everything up."

"Manny, hang on a minute. George is beeping. Wow! It's loud. I'll call you right back."

"Is everything okay?"

George's beeps are deafening. At the top of the stairs, Jane turns and then races to Nana's bedroom. She pushes the door open, sees her mother collapsed on the floor, flushed, soaking in sweat.

"Mom! Oh, God!"

She hears sirens blaring. An ambulance arrives and rushes Nana to New Hope Hospital.

Hours later, Dorrie and Jane are at New Hope Hospital waiting for word on Nana's condition. At nine P.M., Dorrie volunteers to look after Rachel and Sarah. "Don't worry," she comforts Jane.

"Tell them I'll call as soon as I hear anything."

"Here's my cell phone number ... just in case," Dorrie says.

Jane paces the hospital halls until she spots Sam Stone coming through the swinging doors of the Intensive Care Unit. He says Nana is responsive and her vital signs have stabilized.

"Thank God! Do you know what happened?"

"We don't know. She suffered a debilitating shock to her system; plunged her into a comatose state, actually almost like a diabetic coma. We could have lost her."

"Nana has diabetes?"

"That's just it. She doesn't."

"There must be a way to sort this out. Right?"

"Of course. She's in very good hands. She'll be in intensive care all night. Why don't you go home and look after the girls? I'll keep an eye on her."

Jane notices Sam looks uncertain and decides to stay. At dawn, she awakens on a sofa in the deserted waiting room with a very stiff neck. She checks with the duty nurse at the station: no change in Nana's condition. She decides to go home, check in on the girls, and change clothes.

She does her best to reassure her daughters, who are concerned but calm, thanks to Dorrie's steady hand. Jane cancels most of her morning chores before driving back to the hospital.

Something is nagging at her, and she can't put her finger on it. She keeps flashing back to Nana collapsed on the bedroom floor. George's deafening alarm.

She remembers standing there frozen when the EMT guys came up the stairs. Paralyzed with fear.

Paralyzed?

That was it. Jane hadn't dialed 911! Had Nana hit the autodial button on her phone when she began to feel faint? That must be what happened. But the phone was on the far side of the room, still in its cradle.

Maybe Sam had given Nana one of those electronic bracelets doctors use to monitor their patients' vital signs and it automatically sent out an alarm.

Funny, she hadn't noticed it.

Chapter 56

Over the next week, Nana's condition improves—thanks, Sam says, to transfusions and a stream of antibiotics and nutritional supplements. Soon, she's feeling well enough to walk the halls in her plaid housecoat, dropping in on patients, particularly older ones whose families are too scattered or busy to visit. By the second week, she's handing out Dorrie's cookies with the enthusiasm of a candy-striper.

Hospitals are disorientating, even grim places, particularly around the holidays when tinsel and Christmas decorations hang forlornly on the walls.

One afternoon, I stop by and glimpse Nana pressing a handful of bills on a middle-aged woman wearing a coat much too thin for the weather. Not wanting to intrude, I step back into the corridor. A nurse tells me the woman is an outpatient, battling cancer. Nana insisted she take a taxi home.

I'm chatting with Nana when Sam Stone comes by on his rounds.

"We're going to keep you for a few more days. Your labs are inconsistent; your numbers are up, down, all over the chart."

"I'm feeling much better, if that matters."

"We'll both feel better when we get this sorted out." Stone turns and draws a long syringe from a cabinet drawer. "Just an antibiotic to ward off infection. Your immunity may be compromised. And since you refuse to sit and rest, a certain sensitivity is not going to slow you down, is it?"

"Sam, isn't there a pill?"

* * *

The next morning Jane stops by before heading over to the day-care center. She pulls the laptop out of her briefcase. Nana visibly brightens.

"Figured old George here would cheer you up. How're you feeling?"

"Much better."

"You look better. Getting some rest?"

"Sure. Some."

"Got to keep up our strength, right?"

"We do," says Nana.

Jane fiddles with the bedspread. "Mom, can I ask you something? It's kinda been on my mind."

"Yes?"

"Do you remember anything about ... your attack?"

Nana stares out the window, then turns back to Jane. "You know, it's funny, I was just thinking about it myself." She sips from a water cup. "I remember getting a sweater out of my drawer. I was really cold. I guess that was odd, suddenly feeling this terrible chill. Then my legs go all rubbery. The room tilted like that funhouse ride. You know the one?"

"Sure." Jane pauses. "So then you called nine-one-one? Right?"

"No, I never got near the phone. The next thing I remember is waking up in the hospital. I assumed you called the ambulance."

"I see. Were you wearing some sort of electronic monitor, you know, a bracelet?"

Nana holds up her hands. "No."

"But you did hear George, right?"

"No. What about George?" Nana's hand slides protectively over the computer.

"Him beeping?"

"Beeping?"

"Yeah. I was talking to Manny on my cell when I heard this really loud beeping upstairs. Scared the heck out of me. I ran up and found you slumped on the floor. I was terrified. Frozen. Yet it seemed no more than a minute later, the EMT guys are coming up the stairs."

They look at each other.

"So you called them and then lost track of time with all the commotion," Nana says. "Your mind can play tricks on you. And those guys, they come pretty quick."

"I'm pretty sure I didn't. Wait a minute! I still had my cell in my hand when I got upstairs."

"Aha!" Nana says. "Then it must have been Manny. I bet you never hung up! He heard the commotion and called nine-one-one. Goodness, I've got to thank him."

"We must have scared the heck out of him," says Jane.

"What counts is that you guys got help in time. Thank you for saving my life."

Jane is still putting it all together. "You're welcome, but you don't have to thank me. I love you."

"I know you do."

"Mom, if it's okay with you, I've got to get moving. I'll stop by later. Okay?"

"I'm fine, really. Thanks for George."

Nana looks past Jane and sees Sam Stone standing in the doorway. Sam strolls in, trailed by a group of interns.

"George?" he says. "You didn't mention there was a George in your life."

"I didn't?" says Nana. "Would you like to say hello?"

Nana digs the laptop out from under her blankets, presses START.

"See you guys later," says Jane.

"George? Oh, right, George." Sam gives Nana a look. "So George is a computer, a pretty fancy computer. What's with all these little gizmos?"

"Icons. Sam, if you've got a minute, I'll show you some research I've been doing on the Internet."

"I've got just about a minute." Sam peers at George's flashing screen. "Don't you need to hook it up to the phone? The one in my office has a ... a modem."

"George is wireless." Nana points. "You pop in this little card."

"Interesting. May I have a look?"

"Sure. You ever visit WebMD, Sam?"

"I might have." Sam watches George's screen as Nana types.

"There's these other websites I found too," she says.

George's screen flashes.

"Nana, at your age it's not a good idea to go *surfing*. Isn't that the word?" Sam chuckles as he squints at the screen. "Wait a second." He stares at the screen. A few of the bolder interns look over his shoulder. "Hmmm. Do you realize what you've been looking at?"

"Probably not. I don't recognize that address, but my memory these days ..."

Sam taps George's screen. "This is a new leukemia protocol. I didn't know it was in clinical trials."

"Really? This stuff seems to pop up on the computer all the time. I can't make heads or tails of it. You told me not to try to play doctor, remember?"

"I did."

Sam checks his watch. He reviews Nana's charts with the interns, scribbles a few notes.

"Let's discuss this when I have some time. Right now, we're running a little late. We've got another dozen folks to visit. Isn't that right?"

The interns nod vigorously. One of them, a young woman, smiles at Nana. "Looks like interesting research, Mrs. Martin."

"I'll come back this afternoon," Sam says. "I'd like to take a closer look at what you've turned up. Maybe George and I can figure out whether you may qualify for this trial."

"Hopefully." Nana is very curious about this new website.

Sam heads out the door.

"You hear anything from Dom?" Nana calls after him.

"No, not a word."

"Still?"

"I'm sure he'll turn up. Come along, doctors, something tells me we may have stumbled onto something quite interesting."

"Stumbled?" Nana says softly as he goes out the door.

She tries to rest, but her mind is racing. She feels a twinge of dizziness, sits up and tries to clear her head. Her breath grows ragged as if a weight is pressing down on her chest. The digital readouts on her monitors flash. Gasping, she reaches for the pager to call the nurse. Her hands fumble on the sheets. She can't find it! Her hand closes around George. An alarm sounds. Moments later, a nurse rushes into the room. She checks Nana's vital signs, asks some questions, and adjusts the IV on her arm.

"You're all right, dear."

"I'm not. I don't think I am."

"The monitors are reading normal. It could be a side effect of the medications. I'll alert your doctor."

She resets the monitors.

"Please sit with me a minute."

"Of course."

The woman sits down on the side of the bed. She moves George to one side and holds Nana's hand as if taking her pulse. "Autumn Leaves," one of Nana's favorite songs, plays softly out of the computer speakers. The nurse smiles and begins humming along. After a while, Nana drifts off to sleep.

> *Since you went away*
> *the days grow long*
> *And soon I'll hear*
> *old winter's song*
> *But I miss you most of all*
> *my darling*
> *When autumn leaves*
> *start to fall.*

In a dream, Jack Martin whispers to her, his words as soothing as the song. He reaches out to touch her face, to brush the silvered hair off her brow. In her sleep, Nana feels a breeze caress her cheek.

Chapter 57

With Nana hospitalized, Jane has been paying much more attention to the comings and goings of Rachel and Sarah. She's discovering that responsibility provides a bit of certainty in an uncertain time; routine helps ease her fears. The truth is she'd prefer to keep the girls close, but as any parent knows, that's not easy. Tonight, they have sleepovers at friends' houses. Jane delivers them to the doorsteps and waits until a parent answers the bell.

She smiles at her over-protective behavior, wishing Nana could see her.

When she gets home, the house is chilly. She wonders if the pilot light in the furnace has gone out. She doesn't feel like descending into the gloom of the basement. Outside, branches sway in the wind, casting shadows on the walls. The creaks and groans of the old boards—the background music of Jane's childhood—are exaggerated and unnerving as in some cheesy horror movie.

Shivering, she heads upstairs. In the office, she glances at the photograph of her father standing alongside his army tank. It strikes her that the twenty-year-old Jack Martin in the photo, much younger than she is now, had the courage to carry on. Or found the courage, as did Nana, but now Nana is old and ... ill.

Molly chooses this moment to get up from under the desk—the Lab's arthritis has been acting up—and lumbers over to lick Jane's fingers. Tears begin to well.

"I still need you, Dad," Jane says. "Help me figure out what to do."

Jane sobs.

The wind shrieks. Downstairs, the screen door opening onto the back porch slams, startling her. Sarah must have left it unhooked when she let Molly out. She's got to talk to her about that.

Sniffling, Jane picks up a photo on the desk. A smiling toddler waves a pail and shovel at the camera. Looking closely, she can make out the shadow of a man in a baseball cap—Jack Martin's shadow—holding the camera. He'd watched over her every day of her life. She stares at her younger self, thinks about the changes that have unfolded over the years.

Things *were* different then. They were simpler. Families were support systems, not generational battlegrounds. Marriage was not as fragile as the wedding crystal gathering dust in the china cabinet. Small towns were wonderful places, though small towns also concealed sadness, loneliness, and uncertainty.

Responsibility doesn't change. It's no different for Jane than it was for Nana and Jack. Raising children—smart, stubborn, day-to-day, joy-to-joy, crisis-to-crisis children—is not the simple task described in the self-help books, particularly with girls without a father in a town where most kids took Mom and Dad for granted.

Jane knows she has overcompensated. Rachel and Sarah need guidance as well as love. Rachel's hunger for popularity masks a deeper insecurity. Jane doesn't know how to bridge the divide growing between them except by giving in to the teen's whims.

She hasn't made the tough decisions Rachel really needs. And so Rachel suffers. Her grades have toppled since she's become a cheerleader. Jane has considered pulling her out of the cheerleading competition but doesn't have the heart.

Sarah's sweetness is a magnet that can attract both cruelty and kindness. She is becoming willful and curious about a world she has glimpsed mostly on television. Jane has not been conscious of Sarah's vulnerability.

She'll have to find the courage—that's the word, courage—to carry on, to protect her daughters, to be the best mother she can be.

"But it's hard," she whispers to the ghosts in the room.

The phone rings, startling her. It's Sarah. She's forgotten a DVD she wanted to bring to the sleepover.

"Mom, can you bring it by? The girls are counting on me."

Jane frowns at the rain now pattering against the windows. "Sure, honey. I'll get my keys."

Jane is ready to hop in the car when Sarah calls back and tells her, "Never mind, we're going to watch *Dancing with the Stars*. It's the finals."

"You sure?"

"Then we're going to dye my hair jet black."

"What!"

"Just kidding. Thanks, Mom. See you in the morning."

Like millions of women, Jane feels like she just woke up one morning and found herself a wife, then a single parent, a career woman, a baby boomer with an aging parent, twenty other roles. She's been asking herself, "What does this overused notion of 'living in the moment' really mean?" Wandering aimlessly, without responsibility, trying to stretch childhood into forever? Strip away the frills, the *moment* meant being aware, responsible, and vigilant, yet poised to live to the fullest. The concepts are not exclusive, and the moment is always now.

Jack and Nana are holding hands in another photograph. Nana has been the bridge spanning the generations. What if Nana dies?

The answer leaps into Jane's head: "I'm not ready."

In her bedroom, she stares at the cold, distant stars outside her window. She feels the pull of gravity, the tidal ebb and flow of ordinary life, tugging at her. She dreams of other things, beings composed of both darkness and light, swirling around her, reaching out to her.

Chapter 58

The phone jangles at eight A.M. Jane grabs for the receiver, misses, then catches it on the second try.

"Good morning, Rachel," a male voice intones. "Opportunity's calling."

"Rachel isn't here," Jane mumbles. "May I tell her—?"

The connection is lost.

"Hello?"

Jane puts down the receiver. The caller ID reads OUT OF AREA. The phone rings again. She answers, and again the connection is lost.

Weird, she thinks and then remembers how hard the wind was blowing last night; maybe something happened with the lines. Those odd dreams come back to her. She's having her second cup of coffee when the phone rings yet again.

"Jane Martin, please."

"This is she."

It's Robert Derosier calling from the ad agency she queried about creating an image for Happy Kids. He apologizes for calling so early but says he likes to get a head start on the day. They talk for ten minutes. Jane describes her business and the ideas she's been toying with. She tells him she's begun to do background screening on all her employees. She's decided she owes that to the children and their families. Derosier listens, asks a few questions. Before hanging up, he gives Jane an e-mail address and asks her to send him information on Happy Kids and digital photos of her space, her staff, and the kids.

"Send me some stuff on you and your family too. I'm thinking we'll be able to put together a simple but effective branding campaign that will separate you from the competition."

"Family stuff?"

"Sure, you're a good mother. Let's take advantage of that fact."

"Good idea!"

The unease Jane has been feeling slips into the background.

Chapter 59

Jane strolls down Main Street to the New Hope Savings and Loan building. She scans the directory and heads for the offices of Walters & Derosier. Passing through the ad agency's gun-metal gray doors, she finds what had been a traditional oak-and-leather financial-services office transformed into granite and brushed-steel workspace, accented by edgy sculpture and art. These are changes she likes to see in New Hope.

A receptionist, pale as ivory, greets her. After a few minutes, the woman, who resembles an actress—Jane can't place her—ushers her in to Derosier's office.

As the door clicks closed, the woman stops in front of a mirror and brushes a lock of ink-black hair from her face. I've always imagined many faces in that mirror. Ellen Asplund, a teenage runaway from one of New Hope's wealthiest families who died in a terrible tragedy is one, God rest her soul. Shelby is another.

Derosier wears a suit right out of GQ. He's handsome in the world-weary way many women find attractive.

"Thanks for sending over the material. We were able to put together a PowerPoint presentation."

"That was quick! Thanks."

Derosier says he buys into Jane's Happy Kids' concept, "gets the business model," but her ideas need some professional tweaking.

In fact, Jane doesn't have a "model" except to work "really, really hard" providing a good experience to parents and kids. She's very happy to be working with a real marketer.

"Let me show you what we've got."

He walks over to his laptop and projects a series of posters and outdoor billboards—many built around images of Jane and Sarah in front of a group of deliriously happy kids. He proposes a print ad in the Sunday newspaper, an interactive Internet ad, and a TV commercial that will reach parents via local broadcasting.

"By the way, your daughter is fabulous. Just the right look. Where did she get that incredible hair?"

"From her father," Jane says sourly.

Jane is excited. This will definitely trump the advertising Romper-Rhymer has been doing, but then she realizes she can't afford this work. Even purchasing time on local radio stations will be a stretch. She might be able to do some direct mail advertising, maybe stick with a *Weekly Shopper* promotion.

Another opportunity down the tubes, she thinks. *It's the same old story.*

The fact that Nana's "Safe Kids" idea has been downplayed as "too downbeat" goes right by Jane.

"I ... I don't have a real budget. I couldn't pay for this."

"You can't afford not to." He moves away from his desk, walks closer. "I like you, Ms. Martin. I can see that you're a really good person, and I believe in what you're doing."

Jane stares at him, inhales a whiff of his cologne. A little strong for her taste.

"You're wondering why I'm saying this?"

"It's just too far out of my reach," Jane says. "I don't want to play games."

"No games. I'm new in town, so it's right for me to get involved, to fit in, to be part of things. That's how I'll grow my business. It's important that I'm associated with such an important community service, very important."

He goes on to mention pro-bono possibilities, trade-outs, favors he can call in from contacts he has at newspaper and television stations.

"Mr. Derosier," says Jane. "I'm not following."

"Call me Rob. What I'm saying is, let's figure out what you can afford, and I'll cover as much as I can of the rest of it."

"You're kidding, right?"

"It'll be my gift to the community." He looks at Jane. "So you like the concept?"

Jane hesitates, remembering Nana's insistence on a "Safe

Kids" theme. She's about to suggest Rob work it back in and is trying to find a delicate way to say this.

"Something bothering you?" asks Derosier.

"I'll be honest. Things haven't exactly gone my way lately. And now a very talented man I barely know goes out of his way to … to help? I'm wary, I guess. Not too many people I've come across are willing to do something without a lot of dollar signs attached."

"Jane, it's about the work … and giving back."

"But …"

"Happy Kids is a unique opportunity, unless of course you're really uncomfortable with my generosity?"

"No! I'm not saying that."

"Jane, I put this together with *your kids* in mind. Trust me, we'll create a buzz people won't soon forget."

"A buzz about Happy Kids. I'd love it!"

"Say no more. Let me get back to work."

Rob suggests they have dinner the next week to review progress. "How about next Thursday at this new French restaurant near the Market Hotel? I have to meet another client at the hotel conference center later that evening, but I'll make time to do both." He'll bring some sketches and drafts of the ad copy for her to go over. Jane agrees. As she's leaving, she tells Rob she might want some additional copy, maybe a newspaper ad emphasizing the importance of trust and responsibility.

"Couldn't agree more," he says. "Day-care centers are all about trust. How about 'Happy Kids Are Trusting Kids'?"

"That could work! 'Trusting kids'! I like it."

He sees her to the door. When she leaves, Derosier turns to his receptionist. "Trusting kids. What do you think?"

"I was one."

"So was I."

Jane heads to her SUV, walking on air.

"I knew I could trust my instincts!" she says to herself. "Trust, and good things will happen. Wait till I tell Nana!"

She drives to the hospital. There's more good news. Nana tells Jane she's being released! Sam Stone is recommending a new protocol developed at Johns Hopkins, a treatment he learned about working with George. Nana meets the trial criteria, and he hopes to have an approval. Better yet, she can be treated on an outpatient basis.

"That's wonderful!"

"You can pick me up tonight," Nana says. "Five-thirty P.M."

"Are you sure it's not too soon?"

"Are you kidding? They're kicking me out."

Nana is impressed by what Jane tells her about her advertising campaign, though she wonders about the motivation behind this pro-bono stuff.

"I've got to run," says Jane, cutting her off. "See you in couple of hours."

Back at the house, Jane tells Rachel Nana's coming home. She talks about Rob, his fabulous office, and the upcoming ad campaign.

"Want to know the best part? He believes in Happy Kids. Validation from one's peers is so important."

"Mom, I'm in high school. I know!"

Jane giggles. "Rob and I are going to review the work over dinner."

"Go, Mom! Is he cute?"

"I think so, in a European kind of way. Definitely not your quarterback type."

Now it's Rachel's turn to blush. Her popularity has soared since Jamie Kaufmann asked her to the football team's Christmas party. Beneath the jock persona, Jamie is shy, a serious student, and a member of the Fellowship of Christian Athletes. Rachel unfortunately minimizes these traits. She wants to *impress* Jamie. Winning the cheerleading competition will go a long way. That's her purpose!

Soon, Roge will announce the audition schedule for the cheerleading contest. Rachel has been working on her routines nonstop.

Mother and daughter chat happily as they drive over to the hospital to pick up Nana.

Chapter 60

New Hope lies in a blanket of clean snow.

Even at a distance, the house with its pitched roof and gables is unmistakable. Nana and Jane are framed in the office window, Jane typing, Nana sitting next to her, hand resting on her daughter's shoulder.

In her room, restless Rachel fantasizes about the future: cheerleader ... model ... American Idol, her face on the cover of *People* and *US* magazines, her name on everyone's lips. Millions of fans wondering what guys she's dating, what glamorous outfit she'll be wearing at the next Hollywood party.

Next door, Sarah is dreaming peacefully.

The scene, or some variation of it, is playing out in millions of American homes. So many hopes and aspirations, fulfilled and unfulfilled, churn beneath the calm surface of ordinary life; love, concern, good intentions, generosity, all flowing in a great stream under the arch of heaven.

How blessed we are.

And how fragile our peace.

Chapter 61

Nana's energy seems to be returning, though Sam warned that the illness would likely wax and wane. Uncertain how long this phase will last, she decides to stay active. Soon enough, she's back on-line.

When she instant messages Manny her keystrokes practically outpace her thoughts, evidence she really is feeling better.

"Hello Manny!"

"Mrs. Martin! How are you?"

"Thank God, pretty good, I'm getting back up to speed on the computer."

"Great. Stay with it."

"Manny, I want to thank you. You saved my life."

"Oh." He hesitates a half-second. "You're very welcome. Happy to do it."

He's had quite a few people say stuff like this after he's fixed their computers or taught them some basic skills.

"Don't be embarrassed. I mean it."

"I'm not embarrassed. Glad I could be of help." He tries to change the subject. "Hey, you know I'm working with Mrs. Smith. She's my second favorite student."

"Mrs. Smith? Dorrie Smith?"

"She dropped in a couple of weeks ago."

"When I was laid up in the hospital?"

"Right. She said you'd persuaded her to come by. Whoa! Mrs. Martin, could you slow down your typing? I can't keep up!"

"Stop flattering me."

"I'm really not. Oh, and the Gabriels are also taking classes."

"Really? That's very interesting."

"Got to run. Customers are in the room!"

She's massaging her fingers when the phone rings. Dorrie is on her way over.

"You're not driving and talking, are you?" Nana chides. "Twenty-five percent of traffic accidents are caused by distraction."

"My, you are better. I see you're minding everyone's business again."

Over tea, Dorrie tells Nana about the memorial service the town is planning for Joe Adams. She's on the organizing committee. Two hundred people have e-mailed saying they'd attend. Many of Joe's former students are coming back to town.

"I still can't believe it," Nana says. "Joseph Adams taking his own life? How can it be?"

"I don't know."

"I guess it's true what they say," adds Nana. "'You have to walk in another person's shoes.'"

"You think this was about Steve?" Dorrie wonders.

"Deep down, I do." The thought starts her brooding about Jane and the girls. She pushes it away.

"Steve was my student," says Dorrie. "I know he respected his father. He wanted to be like him."

"I don't believe Joe understood that," says Nana. "There's too much misunderstanding, too few families sitting down and talking. If only he'd asked for help."

"That really wasn't Joe's way."

"I know."

Would Jane ask for help? The thought pricks Nana like the point of a knife. She hesitates, then changes the subject.

"So I hear you're taking a computer class."

"Two, actually. Finding that crook in Chicago really convinced me! Also what you were doing and how much good stuff you were learning. Here I am, a teacher! Why the heck didn't I get started years ago? I guess I was afraid that I was too old or too slow. Anyway, I decided I would, well, carry on."

"You had me six feet under?"

"Maybe four. I'm glad you're back. Computers aren't hard. There's nothing to be afraid of, nothing technical, and so much right at your fingertips. In fact, I've actually decided to *start* a class—Connections—e-mails and such, for seniors at the church center. Thursday afternoons. Pastor Richards says he'll join us.

Manny volunteered to get us going."

"My Manny?"

"Is there any other Manny?"

"Did you know he called nine-one-one when I had my attack? He was on the phone with Jane. He heard the commotion and called it in."

"Wow. He *is* your Manny. What luck! Hey, do you want to be a co-teacher?"

"I can do that … provided I'm still kicking on Thursday."

"Provided," says Dorrie with a matching straight face. "It's too much for me all by myself, being old."

The two friends hug and head upstairs.

"Dorrie, I've been thinking more and more about things. We've got to find Dom. We have to talk to him."

"About Joe?"

"About Dom. I'm worried."

"Me too."

Nana shows Dorrie how to access the on-line White Pages, and the two of them try to find a new phone listing for Dominic Palermo. No luck. Nana sends Dom another e-mail.

A hundred miles away, Dom stands outside a rental cottage staring at an ocean as gray and somber as his mood. Dom Palermo, alone on a deserted beach, struggling with regret. Despair eating at him since the day the stranger walked into the diner.

He goes inside, turns on his laptop, and retrieves the photos stored on the hard drive. He stares longingly at the images, actually catches himself trying to touch them. He misses his family so much.

"Enough already!" He walks out to his truck and reaches for the cell phone DJ gave him for emergencies. After fiddling with it, he realizes it's not charged. The moment passes. He tosses the phone back into the glove compartment.

What would I say? he thinks. *That I don't count anymore? And I can't face it?*

He never checks his e-mail.

Chapter 62

On Thursday, Rob Derosier calls to confirm dinner.

"We have reservations. Tonight at seven P.M. La Tour d'Argent at the mall."

"Wow. That place was just featured in *Gourmet* magazine."

"The food is quite good, plus it's accessible to the hotel and conference center. I like to mix business and pleasure."

"That's the way to go. My day-care center is half a block from Lenny's Laundromat. Well, since you mention business, can I stop by to see the finished work? I don't want to wait."

"We're kind of slammed."

"Won't take long. I've got an appointment near your office this afternoon, so maybe I could drop by?"

"I've got client meetings outside the office right up until dinner. Of course, you're welcome to come by and try."

"Thanks. In any event, I'll see you at seven."

"I look forward to it."

At three-thirty P.M., Jane drives home to check on Nana. The girls are out of school—holiday break—and she particularly doesn't want Sarah tiring Nana out. Rachel will have to look after her.

She comes through the door and finds Nana washing dishes.

"Mom, are you feeling well enough to be on your feet?"

"I'm feeling pretty darn good. Eager to get moving."

"Get moving? Didn't I hear Doc Stone tell you to take it easy?"

"As a matter of fact, Sam dropped by with my new medicine this morning. He said I look terrific."

"That's wonderful."

Nana picks up a pill bottle, shakes it. "For the first two weeks, I'm to take a couple of these blue pills, three times a day, then I start on the orange ones. No dizziness or other side effects so far. Thank God."

"I bet it's some super medicine they clone in a laboratory, like interferon or something that seeks out the bad cells and destroys them without messing anything else up."

"I don't know. You know, I'm always complaining to Sam about medical care, but it's amazing what they can do. I sure wish ..."

She looks away.

"You're thinking about Daddy, aren't you?"

"How did you know?"

"Don't. There's no purpose ... except that Daddy would want you to take good care of yourself."

"I know that, and I will."

And then, to Jane's utter shock, Nana tells her she's planning to go out.

"Dorrie and I have started a computer class. We're teaching the first session at the church center later this afternoon."

"Mom!"

"It'll just be for a couple of hours. After all those days cooped up in the hospital, I need some human contact. I'll be home by seven."

"Okay," Jane says carefully. "Note that I'm not telling you how to live your life."

"Noted. And thank you."

"I'll leave dinner for you guys on the stove."

"I can fix something."

"No, you can rest."

Nana finishes up at the sink. She walks over and puts a hand on Jane's shoulder.

"I know you're concerned, but I really am feeling much better. Maybe the pills are working. Maybe it's just good to be home ..."

"I hope so."

"... but I do know I can't sit around like an invalid. That *will* kill me."

"I ... understand. I just worry."

"Don't."

"Please stay off your feet until it's time."

Nana nods. "I think I'll take a nap."

Jane whips up a casserole then jogs upstairs to select the right outfit for the fabulous French restaurant Rob has chosen. She checks her watch. She's got to make her five P.M. appointment at Giorgio's Salon.

Jane smiles as she reaches for a pale blue skirt that shows off her shapely legs. Rachel skips into the bedroom, her eyes caked with makeup, waving a printout of an e-mail.

"Tonight's the night! Roge just confirmed my appointment."

"Not with that face." Jane immediately regrets her words as hurt registers in her daughter's eyes. "I'm sorry. I think you're wearing too much makeup. Okay?"

"Okay."

"Where's Sarah?"

"Playing upstairs. I didn't want her to wear Nana out."

"Appointment?" Jane says as an alarm bell begins to tinkle. "What appointment? Honey, can we start over?"

Rachel explains breathlessly that tonight is the "really big" audition for the cheerleading scholarship.

"Seven-thirty in the Evergreen Ballroom. They're going to set up the place to shoot videos, just like MTV! You can drive me, right? You promised."

"I …" Jane hesitates. "I didn't know it was tonight."

"It is. I just found out." Rachel waves the printout. "Mom?"

Jane takes a breath. "Okay, it's just that …"

Rachel notices the dressy outfit Jane is holding. "Tonight's your big date, isn't it?"

"It's actually a business dinner."

"What about Nana?"

"She's napping. Later on, she and Dorrie are going over to the church for a couple of hours. You can ask her when she gets up."

Jane checks her watch. She can see the complications growing like a run in a stocking. She was counting on Rachel to keep an eye on Sarah and Nana.

"I can't believe we both have appointments on the same night. Oh, well." Jane drops her skirt on the bed.

"Mom, I'm sorry!"

Rachel had received the preliminary date days ago. In fact, she knew it conflicted with Jane's business dinner but decided there were advantages to appearing at the competition without her mom. The same went for her grandmother.

"I know it's not your fault. It's just ..."

"Hey! I can catch a ride with Betty and her mom."

"Betty?" says Jane, surprised to feel a tingle of an old competitiveness. She and Claire Edwards, Betty's mom, were New Hope High cheerleaders twenty years ago.

"Betty's in it too? Why didn't you tell me?"

"I forgot. Her mom e-mailed Roge weeks ago after I mentioned the competition in the cafeteria. You know how pushy Mrs. Edwards can be."

"Believe me, I do."

Rachel's plan is the only way to avoid an explosion when Jane got a look at the skimpy borrowed outfits and a few other details she has packed in her suitcase.

"Please let me work this out," Rachel says. She pauses, lip quivering, a move she's practiced for her close-ups. "You're always telling me to exert a little independence."

Jane hesitates, then, "Okay."

Rachel rushes over and hugs her. "You're the greatest mom ever!"

"Call Claire Edwards, then wash off that makeup, okay?"

Rachel grabs Jane's cell phone and skips out of the room.

Jane checks her watch. She's got to get moving.

Betty's line is busy, and Rachel decides she can work this minor detail out later.

"All set, Mom!" she announces. "Mrs. Edwards will pick me up around seven. Betty's appointment is ... right after mine."

"Good. Don't leave until Nana gets back. And don't forget to let me know how it goes. Okay?"

"No problem! I'm so excited!"

"So am I."

Rachel is amazed at how easily these stories roll off her tongue. Ride or no ride, she's not missing her chance at fame. No way!

After Jane leaves, Rachel does get through to Betty Edwards. There's a problem. Betty's audition is scheduled for the *following* evening. She'll have to find another ride. Jamie can probably drive her. If all else fails, she can take a bus over to the mall. It's all good. She'll do whatever it takes.

Chapter 63

All Hallows Church Hall. Twenty seniors sit in front of a row of computers Dorrie has persuaded the school board to donate. It is the least they can do after almost causing her to lose her retirement funds.

Nana gives Manny a hug the moment he walks through the door. After the usual round of delays to refill coffee cups and make last-minute trips to the restrooms, Nana describes her peculiar introduction to computers, how she didn't appreciate George at first, but now the machine is indispensable, a window that "puts the world at my fingertips."

She describes how e-mails work, how the software automatically saves other people's addresses so you only have to type them once, how family pictures and home movies can be sent anywhere in seconds, how you can pay bills without stamps, play solitaire or your favorite songs, monitor your health, track down a high school classmate or a guy you served with in the army.

Dorrie follows Nana with a lesson on Internet awareness. She warns the group that there are dangers as well as opportunities in cyberspace—fake solicitations from "temporarily" impecunious heirs of immense overseas fortunes, willing to share their largesse for a small investment, miracle cures, phony contests and "free" prizes, imaginary charitable appeals, false financial websites masquerading as legitimate ones intended to trick consumers into providing passwords—scams run by clever con artists who prey on the loneliness and trusting nature of senior citizens.

"I know what you're thinking," Nana says when Dorrie winds up. "'Too complicated and risky.' Trust me, it's as easy as turning on a light. Safe too, provided you follow a few common-sense rules. And it's definitely not only for youngsters. Our generation can't afford to miss this train."

As Nana talks, Manny passes out registration forms and a clever brochure—*Computers: A Real Lifesaver For Seniors*—that lists "Ten Do's and Don'ts for Beginners" he put together. He introduces himself, volunteers to help with any problems or concerns, and blushes when the group applauds.

Everyone is interested—or at least curious. They fiddle with the machines, ask dozens of questions while Manny, Dorrie, and Nana move around, looking over their shoulders. These exchanges go on and on.

In the excitement Nana forgets time is passing.

Chapter 64

Jane exits Giorgio's and walks to her SUV, conscious of the appreciative looks men cast in her direction. She was able to change clothes at the salon and gained a little time. She drives down Main Street to the offices of Walters & Derosier. She parks, digs for change for the parking meter, then gives up. She can't wait to see her ads. She hurries up to the second floor office, rings the bell.

No answer. She tries again.

"Darn!"

A security guard walks by, checking doors. He peers into a closet as Jane walks past him. A gilt sign leaning against the wall reads R.P. GREENLEAF ESQ. REGISTERED FINANCIAL PLANNER. He shrugs, picks the sign up, and drops it into a trash barrel the cleaning people have left in the hall.

Jane heads downstairs. On the sidewalk, she pulls a parking ticket from behind her windshield wipers, tucks it into her glove compartment, and speeds off.

At the house, the phone rings. Rachel grabs it. It's Roge! She hangs up, eyes shining, checks her make-up for the fifth time, struts in front of the mirror. She grabs her bag, heads downstairs.

"Nana?"

To her surprise, no one answers.

"Nana?"

She finds Sarah in the living room watching TV. Molly is licking the dirty dish on the floor next to her.

"Where's Nana?"

"She just called and said she's running late, but Nana can't run!"

"Stop trying to be funny!"

"I wasn't! I told Nana it was okay 'cause you're here."

"Oh, God!" Rachel checks her watch. "Did she say how late?"

"Back by eight," Sarah says. "In case you're even interested, Nana said she was feeling fine."

"Eight!" Rachel races upstairs to her room, calls Jamie

Kaufmann for the third time. "Please pick up!"

No answer. She'd convinced herself Jamie would have no choice but to help even if she called him at the last minute. Wasn't he her hero?

Rachel begins to panic. She runs back downstairs.

"Will you be okay until Nana gets back? I've got to go out. My audition is at seven-thirty. I've got to get going."

"I'm afraid," Sarah moans, pretending to shiver. "Mom says I can never be home alone. You'll be in big trouble."

Rachel's mind is racing. "I've got a better idea! If you promise to behave you can take the bus with me to the cheerleading competition, then we can go Christmas shopping for Mom and Nana."

"For Molly too?"

"Sure."

Rachel rips a scrap of paper from the notepad by the phone. She scribbles something. In her haste, she knocks the phone off the receiver.

Chapter 65

Snow flurries dance as Rachel and Sarah get off a city bus outside Temptation Mall. Christmas music blares from loudspeakers. Santas ring bells alongside cardboard chimneys, soliciting contributions.

Rachel checks her watch. She darts past crowds of shoppers, rushes toward the hotel entrance. Sarah, big-eyed at this unexpected adventure, lags behind. Rachel can't be late. First impressions are so important. She imagines Dottie Rice trashing her right now, playing up to poor Roge. She'll show that creep she had what it takes to be famous.

"Come on!" She turns and grabs at Sarah, who twists and breaks away.

Sarah slips and falls in the slush on the parking lot.

"My new coat! Mom's going to kill you."

Rachel pulls a cell phone from her pocket, punches in a number.

The Market Hotel's neon-and-glass façade beckons.

Chapter 66

La Tour d' Argent. Jane finds Derosier waiting for her at the bar. Awkwardly, she shakes his hand. The smell of his cologne intermingles with a new smell: alcohol.

As they are seated at a candle-lit banquette, Derosier slips a leather briefcase under the table.

"Tonight couldn't come soon enough," Jane says. "I dropped by your office earlier. I knew you wouldn't be there, but ..."

"I'm sorry I missed you. I was with a client, a very demanding fellow." A shadow passes over Derosier's face. He waves—impolitely, to Jane's thinking— to the waiter hovering nearby and orders champagne.

"Is he here in New Hope?"

"For a while. Depends how things go. He might be willing to help support the Happy Kids campaign."

"Really? He's heard about Happy Kids?"

"I mentioned the good work you do."

"How sweet."

The champagne arrives. As the sommelier fills their glasses with a flourish, Jane bubbles on about plans for the center, her hopes for her daughters, how she's heard the *Tournedos Rossini* is terrific. When she catches a breath, she senses Derosier is distracted. She swears he is willing himself to stay seated. He ignores the *foie gras* and glances at his watch.

Rude, Jane thinks. She does her best to carry the conversation. She asks Rob where he grew up. Does he have children?

"Divorced. Don't see the kid, thanks to my ex-wife."

"I'm so sorry. My ex ..."

"No big deal. I focus on the business."

Jane nods. "I understand."

"You do? That's good."

"I think so. I was about to say my ex is a real loser."

A waiter hesitates then approaches the table. "*Madam ...*

Monsieur? Si vous ..."

Derosier waves him off, then stiffens. He reaches inside his jacket for his buzzing phone, stares at the screen.

"I must take this," he says, downing his champagne. "It's important. I've worked on this for months. I wish I could tell you more." His smile is brief and, Jane senses, without humor. "Could take a while, maybe you'd like ..."

"I understand. I'm not your most important client. It's really okay."

The waiter backs away.

"When I get back, we'll go over the work. That's why you're here, isn't it?"

"Yes, it is."

"*Reste ici.* I'll be right back. The campaign is *fantastic!*"

He hurries out of the booth, phone to his ear. Jane watches him hurry under the brighter lights at the center of the restaurant.

"Okay," she reminds herself. "It's not a date. It's a business meeting. Stuff happens." She's killed time in much worse places.

She remembers Rachel hasn't called. Darn it. Jane shrugs at the hovering waiter, reaches for the menu.

Ten minutes pass. She nibbles at her lobster and bay-scallop salad with herb balsamic vinaigrette. Jane reaches into her bag for her phone. It's ten minutes till eight. She'll check in on Nana. Make sure Rachel got to her appointment on time.

Her cell phone is not there. She fumbles inside her handbag.

"Rachel," she says aloud, "tell me you didn't take my phone."

Embarrassed, she borrows a cell from the maitre d' and calls home. Busy. She tries her cell. No answer.

She goes through the entrées a third time, puzzling out some of the more obscure offerings with her beginner's French. She's sliding out of the booth, about to walk over to the public phone by the restroom when she spots Rob's briefcase under the table. She fights the urge to peek and loses.

She looks around one last time, then reaches down and places the briefcase alongside her on the banquette. It's unlocked. She opens it, reaches inside, and pulls out a folder stuffed with bills, rental car receipts, a lease, and some flyers for a photography studio in Austin, Texas.

"Where are my ads? ... Ah, here we go!"

She pulls a manila envelope from the bottom of the briefcase. Inside, she finds a stack of eight-by-ten photos depicting heavily made-up teenagers in sexy underwear and very skimpy tops. A few are no older than Sarah! Their eyes are vacant, empty.

"My God!"

She tears through them, frantically tossing them like playing cards.

A smiling picture of Rachel stares at her.

Chapter 67

Fighting a panic terrible beyond imagining, Jane rushes toward the restaurant's gilded doors. As the waiter and maitre d' stand aghast, she runs out into the mall. Gasping, she enters the Market Hotel's soaring atrium, frantically looking for signs for the Evergreen Ballroom, drawing concerned glances from passersby.

There, a sign, just ahead! Jane pulls open the ballroom's double doors and finds a custodial crew cleaning up after a banquet. Except for them, the cavernous room is completely deserted. She runs up to the workers.

"The cheerleading contest!" she gasps. "Is this the place?"

A few of the crew members look up from their work.

"The contest! My daughter is ..."

"Ma'am," one of them says, "nothing like that is going on around here. Leastways, not tonight. Try the Magnolia Ballroom on the Third Level."

"No! I'm sure it's the Evergreen. I'm sure."

"You might want to check the Events monitor. Back down the corridor toward the lobby on the right."

He senses Jane's distress. "If you want, I can call the concierge."

"Thank you!"

The man pulls out a phone and dials. "Sorry. The line is busy."

Jane, suppressing a scream, turns and races into the corridor. She scans the Upcoming Events listings on a TV screen above her head. Nothing! She frantically begs a cell phone from a group of businessmen.

"Please, I've got an emergency!"

A man hands her his phone. Jane dials 911, but she's too panicked to say very much to the police operator, who keeps urging her to calm down and speak clearly.

Despite the dispatcher's warning to stay on the line, Jane hangs up.

At the house, Nana is coming through the front door. She calls upstairs to the girls and gets no response.

"Rachel? Sarah? I'm home."

Silence. She moves to the foot of the stairs.

"Rachel!"

She can't believe Jane would allow the girls to leave the house at night. Sarah hadn't mentioned a thing about it when Nana called to say she was running late.

She hangs her coat in the hall closet and realizes the kids' coats are missing.

"Where could they have gone?"

Uneasy, Nana walks into the kitchen and spots a note under a magnet on the refrigerator. She's reaching for her reading glasses when she notices the phone is off the hook. She places it on the receiver.

The phone jangles immediately. "Lord!" She stares at an unfamiliar number, deciding whether or not to answer. It rings and rings and rings.

"Hello?"

"Mom!" Jane whimpers. "Mom!"

"Janie? What's wrong?"

"Rachel. I'm at the mall. I've got to find Rachel. Rachel's in trouble! Someone may be trying to hurt her."

"What?"

"Please, I'll explain later. I need Claire Edwards's number. It's unlisted, but it's in the computer. Hurry!"

"Jane, what is happening? Where are you?"

Jane catches her breath. "At the Market Hotel. It's okay. It's gonna be okay. Let me talk to Sarah."

Silence.

Nana pulls the note from the refrigerator door.

"Mom? Mom!"

"Sarah is not here. She's with Rachel."

"My God!"

"They took the bus to the mall."

Numb. Jane hands back the phone, staggers away.

"Jane, are you there? Jane!"

Silence.

Nana climbs the stairs, grim determination on her face. Her cubs are in danger, and she must protect them. She hurries to the computer. George is already running. Her fingers stab at the keys. Screens begin to flash before her eyes. She stands and pulls a photo from the wall, quickly disassembling its frame. She types and moves to another screen. George is *racing*. Nana carefully loads the photo into Jane's scanner and sends the file to the New Hope Department of Public Safety.

Ten minutes later, an Amber Alert—with names, addresses, and digital photos of Sarah and Rachel—comes from the police department to all the restaurants, department stores, and boutiques in the mall, along with radio and TV stations.

One of the businessmen flags a guard. It's Officer John Stanley, working security at the hotel in his off hours. Stanley chases after Jane and radios the mall's security office.

At the house, Nana calls Jane back. A stranger answers. Confused, Nana dials Dorrie.

"Dorrie, get over here right away. Please!"

"Are you all right?"

"No!"

* * *

Holiday music fills the air. Officer Stanley is escorting Jane, who is near hysteria, through the lobby to the hotel manager's office. They pass the Snooty Hooty boutique. Suddenly, Jane bolts and runs into the shop.

Rachel is standing in front of a full-length mirror modeling a skimpy top, smiling at her own image.

"Rachel!"

"Mom?"

Jane looks for Sarah. "Sarah!"

Sarah is not with Rachel.

Chapter 68

The boutique. Rachel is so shocked she turns and runs head-long to the back of the store, startling the sales clerks on their break. Jane races after her.

"What are you doing here?" she bleats. "Mom, you're crying! Did something happen to Nana?"

"I went to the ballroom. Empty! Oh, my God! Where is your sister?"

"Oh? She's ... she's with Roge. He said my outfits didn't work for what he had in mind—'too small-town.' Told me to run down here and pick up something crazy. Told me to charge it to his room. He's going to take pictures of Sarah too."

"Where!"

"Mom, what's wrong?"

"Where is she?" Jane grabs Rachel by the shoulders. She fights the urge to shake her and never stop.

Stanley steps between them. "Let me speak to Rachel."

Rachel registers the policeman for the first time. Now, she's really scared.

"Roge moved the auditions to the penthouse suite. Betty's audition is tomorrow. I'm the last contestant tonight."

Stanley whispers into his radio.

"His name isn't Roge!" Jane sobs.

"What?"

"It's Robert!"

"Robert?"

Rachel fumbles in her pocket and pulls out a plastic card. "Mom, I've got the key. The penthouse."

Again, Stanley keys his radio. "The penthouse," he says, turning his back.

Jane grabs the key and races for the bank of elevators.

"Mom!"

"Mrs. Martin!" Stanley shouts. "Wait!"

Jane darts into a glass cage as the door closes, Rachel trailing behind her. She hits the PH button, and the car ascends, like a bubble in a fish tank, through the hotel's open atrium. Far below, Officer Stanley pounds the elevator call buttons.

Jane stands gasping. Rachel shrinks into a corner.

If you've ever experienced such a moment, you know terror can cause your life to pass before your eyes, literally deconstructed into critical moments, choices, and consequences.

Despite the warnings, despite Nana's many attempts to reach her, Jane understands how blind she was—that she "meant well" was not enough. That she's a "good mother" is not good enough. Terrible things happen to good people all the time. Jane's love for her daughters is incomplete if she does not educate and protect them; that she trusts them is meaningless if she leaves them vulnerable to those who make a mockery of trust.

The pneumatic hiss of the elevator underscores the profound isolation Jane is feeling. Waves of emotion, memories, flashbacks to her childhood, and scenes of her recent life wash over her; illusions and denials are stripped away as the floors crawl by.

What Jane is experiencing is beyond words, beyond guilt, remorse, or exhortations to do better. The landscape is that of the soul's painful journey toward understanding. As in life, the end of the elevator's climb can signal death and despair or new hope. If harm has come to Sarah, Jane is lost.

The elevator hisses to a halt. Jane races down the hall. Rachel points to a set of ornate double doors. Jane slides the card into the suite's electronic lock, hears the click, and rushes inside.

Music pounds! The huge living room has been converted into a photographer's set, its backdrop depicting a squad of cheerleaders prancing across a field. Three outsized computer monitors display images of scantily dressed, preening teenagers drawn from popularkidz.net.

Another monitor displays photos of Rachel and Sarah—the Amber Alert directing security and police to the mall! The images are duplicates of photographs hanging in Nana's office. Yet another monitor carries a closed circuit picture of police moving through the mall, in the hotel lobby, the elevators, on the stairs. Images "Roge" must surely have been monitoring.

Roge is gone.

Rachel and Jane stand speechless, deafened by the sound and the images.

"Mom! Look! It's him!"

Rachel points to one of the monitors. A panicked Robert Derosier races thorough the mall's parking lot, carrying an over-size canvas bag. He unlocks a dark van, looks around, gets in, and roars away.

Jane sinks to her knees.

"Sarah," she whimpers. "Please, God."

Moments pass.

"YES!" A shout cuts through the background noise.

Jane and Rachel race into the suite's master bedroom.

"Mom! Rachel!" Sarah yells. "Come watch!"

She's twirling a cheerleader's baton. She tosses it toward the ceiling and catches it neatly as it comes down. Jane notices the silver cross around Sarah's neck flashing in the incandescent light.

* * *

When Nana and Dorrie arrive, the suite is crowded with investigators. Nana takes in the scene, stares at the images on the monitor, notices the popularkidz.net website she never mentioned to Jane. She sees Rachel clinging to her mother and the tears staining Jane's silk blouse, a nurse talking quietly to Sarah in a corner, Sarah nodding gravely. A wave of shame sweeps over her, leaving her unsteady.

"Why didn't I ...?"

Jane spots Nana. "Mother!"

She rushes across the room and grabs Nana, who is now on the verge of collapse.

"Mother!"

"I should have ..."

"Those are our photographs!" Jane blurts. "How?"

Nana stares at the monitor. "I ... I sent them."

"You?"

"And George."

It turned out that after Sarah disappeared at the mall last summer, Nana looked into the new rapid response systems developed for when, God forbid, a child abduction occurs. She learned lots of malls, supermarkets, and department stores have them. Temptation Mall was among the first to install the high-tech alerts.

Nana points at the monitors. "It's called an Amber Alert. When you called, I ran upstairs, got on-line and scanned the photos as fast as I could and ... sent one to the police."

Jane stares at Nana. "That's what saved us. You're what saved us!"

"No. It didn't have to come to this," Nana says. "I could have ... I should have ..."

"Mom, don't! *You* were right all along. I ignored you. I didn't listen even when I realized I needed help. When you were in the hospital, I felt so lost. I wanted to do what's right. Crazy as it seems, I even reached out to Dad for help. Oh, my God, why didn't I listen?"

"Jane." Nana's voice is almost a whisper. "I often talk to your father in prayer. I know he hears me. I sense him, more and more, trying to protect us. I'm convinced he's watching over us. Now, always."

Chapter 69

Driving home, Nana, Jane, Rachel, and Sarah are silent, each lost in her own version of what had happened and what it meant.

They pass through the unlocked front door, shedding coats and scarves, moving about the kitchen. Music is playing softly in the background.

... A time to be born, a time to die
... A time to heal, a time to laugh ...

Nana grasps the source. She climbs the stairs, Jane and the girls following behind. George. As the lyrics echo through the house, images move across his screen: Nana and Jack, Jane and Rachel, Sarah at her recital, a dozen others—a collage of love, hope, and ultimately, family.

Jane whimpers then, heart bursting, begins to sob. Nana and the girls wrap their arms around her until the spasms pass. Much later, Jane walks the exhausted girls to their bedroom. She tucks them in, hugging each child desperately.

There are no more arguments swirling in Jane's head, no justifications or attempts to downplay the truth: yes, the world seethes with joy and possibility but also with dread and risk, a fact ignored at the peril of those you love.

She walks into Nana's bedroom. She stares at her mother, lying exhausted on her bed.

"Mom, are you awake?"

"Yes."

"Mom, I don't know how you ... how you do what you do," she whispers, "but you always manage. I want to learn from you. I know you won't always be here. I hate the thought, but it's the truth. Someday, Rachel and Sarah will have to go on without me. It's so important that I teach them so they can teach their children."

"But that's how it always is," Nana says. "It's the circle of life."

Her smile is so full of joy it triggers a fresh river of tears from Jane.

"It's how it has to be," Nana says. "Our purpose."

She looks out the window at a star glimmering against the black velvet of the night.

"Under heaven, right?" Jane's smile sparkles amidst her tears.

Chapter 70

It was no coincidence that the understanding that passed between Nana and Jane came at Christmastime, when the light of hope emerges from darkness and renews the world. New Hope's churches were full that season. Families and friends gathered to celebrate and—more than in previous years, it seemed—to remember those less fortunate. It was a true Christmas, a renewal of faith as the Bible tells us, "He sent His Word, and healed them." (Psalms 107:20)

On Christmas morning, a blanket of fresh snow covered the town and the valleys beyond. In the old house, joy flowed like a river. When I arrived at Nana's after services, the smell of roast turkey, ham, and sweet potatoes, the perfume of the fir tree, the faces of my dear friends, filled me with a kind of joyful exhilaration.

I was at the table when the doorbell unexpectedly rang. It was Sam Stone. I saw Nana stiffen behind her smile and Jane move quickly to her side, heard her whisper, "Don't worry, Mother. It will be okay. We will be okay."

"This cannot wait!" Sam said, shedding his coat and hat. He walked up to Nana, grinning, I swear, like a jolly old elf.

"I've a present for you. Apparently the lab technicians worked last night."

He pulled a sheet of paper out of his pocket, unfolded it, and slipped on a pair of glasses.

"Your blood work came back. It looks very good. Red blood count is normal. Your lymphocytes, those are white blood cells, have returned to within normal limits—in fact, on the good side of normal."

"It's incredible." Jane was the first to speak. "Isn't it?"

"My buddy ran the work himself."

Nana sagged, seemed about to fall. Rachel steadied her and helped her to a chair. Nana favored Rachel with that wonderful smile. The rest of us murmured prayers of thanks. A moment later we were clinking glasses. How thin the line separating joy from heartache. A shiver passed thorough me.

"Was it the medicine?" Jane finally asked. "Had to be, right? The powerful new treatment?"

Sam was silent a moment. "It's ... unlikely. Normally, it takes weeks to see progress. I didn't want to tell Nana that. I left some room for other ... possibilities."

I eagerly jumped in at this point. "You're saying her response is beyond scientific expectation?"

"Reverend, keep in mind we never had a firm diagnosis of acute lymphocytic leukemia. It certainly looked like it symptomatically, mind you. Nana was very sick, but somehow she fought whatever it was ... fought hard, and well, in the process, homeostasis, well, equilibrium, seems to have been restored."

"You mean she drove it off?" I asked.

"I wouldn't use that phrase, but I guess I'm not too old or stubborn to realize hard science and miracles have a lot in common."

"Praise God!" I shouted. "Praise God."

Everyone joined in. Is not the birth of a Savior a time of miracles?

Sam and Rose were heading up to their cabin for a few days. Jane packed them a basket of turkey, trimmings, and a pumpkin pie. I took the opportunity to stick my old King James Bible inside. Sam later confided he eventually read every passage.

Chapter 71

Another miracle was quietly unfolding.

Christmas morning, Dom Palermo peered through the curtains of the rental cottage. Escape had become just another kind of prison. Dom could not outrun the pain. Separation from his family, particularly on Christmas, had just made it worse.

Snowflakes floated like lace in the air, stirring long-ago memories of Big Dom and Dom's mother, Gloria, his brothers and sisters gathered at the dinner table. The hurt was so intense it doubled him over. He was suffocating! Gasping, he threw the curtains apart, and a shaft of sunlight broke through the clouds, turning the dark ocean radiant. To Dom the sign was as certain as a star in the East. Then he knew neither fear nor uncertainty—no force on God's good earth—would keep him from his loved ones this Christmas Day.

From the depths of despair, the Spirit—it could have been nothing else—lifted Dom like a rising tide. He dressed, packed his meager bag then grabbed the cell phone in the glove compartment. Yes, it was still dead.

"Idiot!" he berated himself.

He carried the phone into the cottage and plugged it into the charger, never realizing that, unlike a dead auto battery, it was instantly usable. While he waited, he would boot up the computer and send a message to DJ.

To his delight, he heard, "You've got mail."

"Wow, a lot of mail."

He put on his reading glasses, clicked on Nana's e-mails.

"Oh, dear God!" He read about Joe Adams, recalling the night he'd seen his friend wandering alone in a downpour, so many other nights. He could only imagine what Joe had been feeling.

"Joe, I'm so sorry. So sorry."

At that moment, he noticed the indicator bars on the cell phone glowing. Instinctively, he grabbed it and dialed.

Sally, his daughter-in-law answered, exclaiming, "Merry Christmas, Dad!"

"How did you ...?"

"Caller ID!"

Dom could hear the delight in her voice, could feel it was because of his call. After a minute, DJ grabbed the phone.

"Dad!"

"Merry Christmas, son!" Dom shouted. "I love you so much."

Dom didn't care that he was crying. This was his son.

"Merry Christmas, Dad. Oh, to hear your voice! I was feeling so ... You know what I mean?"

"I do. I do, son."

That conversation would replay in Dom's head for the rest of his life.

"I know we've argued," DJ said. "I didn't take your feelings into account. I want to put it aside. Our relationship is more important than what happens with the diner. I realize that. Please come home to us."

"We'll talk about the diner another time, son. It's not important right now. It's Christmas. How's my little guy?"

"Nicky can't wait to see Grandpa ... I'm making lasagna! What time will you be here? We've got your presents under the tree. We prayed you'd come home for Christmas."

"It'll take me a little while."

"We'll wait. Nicky misses his *nonno*. He's right here."

"Nicky boy, Grandpa's coming home!"

"*Sono un ragazzo felice*," he remembered Nicky shouting. "I'm a happy kid!"

Ten minutes later, Dom's pickup roared away from the coast. He stopped one time, to pray at a Nativity scene outside a white clapboard church.

Chapter 72

That Christmas season ended with some sad notes too. Joe Adams's death cast a pall on us. If you've ever suffered loss in your life, you know what I mean about the void that somehow must be filled. The fact that a monster like Derosier or DeWalt—we still weren't sure who he really was—had moved among us unnoticed for months, that he'd come so close to doing terrible harm, that he'd escaped, haunted us.

We tried to put it behind us. The town fathers scheduled Joe's memorial service for the first Monday of the New Year. Sergeant Steve Adams, who fell serving our country, would be honored with his father.

I believe sacrifice gives meaning and importance to life, and it's usually the ordinary people, the Nanas, Dorries, and Doms of the world, whose instinctive kindness and compassion—the Nativity story made flesh—keep mankind moving forward.

In Hebrew, there is a term, *tikkun olam*. It means "repairing the world," a never-ending obligation that brings transformation in human lives. Without getting too far ahead of my story, I will tell you that Jane soon revived Nana's "Happy Kids Are Safe Kids" tagline for her advertising campaign. It was an immediate success, won many awards, and was picked up ("Pro-bono," Jane insisted) by dozens of day-care operations, among whom Jane had become a popular spokesperson on child-safety issues around the country.

Rachel, whose adolescent disregard for the risks inherent in cyberspace brought the family to the very brink of tragedy, later discovered that the e-mail and images she'd thoughtlessly submitted to popularkidz.net, Roge's "social networking" site, had a life of their own, echoed and distorted over time. She was never able to completely erase this electronic footprint, but it became the basis for a powerful lesson she used over the years to protect other vulnerable young people. Only a loving God could transform insecurity into a lifelong desire to care for and safeguard others.

And I will tell you that Jane Martin encountered Shelby years later, ravaged by addiction and despair. And it was Jane who comforted and helped Shelby onto the path of recovery—where she remains.

I imagine the Pale Man, who hated Christmas, absent; his malignant power countered by *communitas*, the spirit of togetherness that binds all societies together.

Chapter 73

I have an old book. There, on the top shelf of my library. My hands tremble when I reach for it, once with dread, now with infirmity. It recounts a parallel story to the promise of Creation and Redemption, a tale of horror and woe that spread and shadowed much of human history

Over the millennia, I believe the Pale Man came to exist—to the degree that he could understand himself—to poison happiness. Corrupt, he lusted after innocence. This is what he did.

As I look back to that long-ago season, certain things become clear. The Pale Man, for all his power, could not foresee his own defeat. Pride blinded him to a Greater Power and to the strength God grants ordinary men and women.

For all his guile, the Pale Man could not know the mind of God. Or comprehend that God's love, *caritas*, delivered through human love and *charity*, is an impenetrable shield. By embracing this Divine gift, the least among us will triumph over the Pale Man.

The Pale Man followed human events closely and understood there were moments—the enormous technological and cultural transformation at the beginning of the twenty-first century being one of them—that tore a gap in the fabric of existence and left mankind insecure and uncertain.

He was watchful and patient.

He returned to New Hope in the shadow of the New Year.

Chapter 74

The man who fled the Market Hotel slips unnoticed into the line of parents waiting to pick up their children at New Hope Elementary School. He sits there, the van replaced by a gleaming yellow sports car, his face hidden behind mirrored glasses. In the passenger's seat snuggles a puppy with a bright pink collar. He inches to the front of the line, eager to take his pleasure, eager to inflict a loss from which New Hope will not recover.

I imagine the Pale Man watching.

Nana and Dorrie are driving up the street.

He sees the red-haired girl skipping down the steps. He unlocks the passenger door, eases the car into gear. Time slows as if unwilling to countenance what is happening. He moves the car forward.

Now he has her attention. Sarah smiles at the shar pei, its wrinkly muzzle pressed against the passenger window, front paws pattering against the glass. Sarah approaches the car, taps the window with her knuckle.

"How cute!"

One moment more ...

Dorrie noses the big Buick in front of him.

"Sarah!"

Sarah hesitates, waves goodbye to the dog.

"Nana! Aunt Dorrie. You guys are early."

The man floors, then jerks the car to a halt, tires screeching. Sarah yelps in fear and backs away. Heads swivel. The police officer assigned to the school starts to walk over. Nana stares into the emptiness behind the sunglasses. He finds himself riveted by her gaze. He must break away. He roars out of line into the oncoming traffic as the officer reaches for his radio.

At that instant, Dom Palermo comes cruising down the street. He's humming an aria as he heads back over to DJ's house. He's been doing some thinking. DJ's investor may have vanished, but Dom has some ideas of his own about, well, an Elite Two Diner.

A low-slung yellow car, tires smoking, swerves in front of him. Dom's reflexes are not what they once were. He rams the vehicle broadside, drives it across the street into a brick wall.

"Sweet Jesus!" Dom exclaims.

Bleeding, the man staggers from the wreckage. Dom, unhurt, gets out of the truck to offer assistance; he recognizes the miserable creature hobbling toward him. The arrogance and cruelty are gone, replaced by fear. "You!" the man says.

Dom draws back, hesitates, then moves forward to help. "Take it easy."

The man staggers. "Save me!" he whispers.

Nana approaches. A wave of pity sweeps over her.

"Please."

Did the Pale Man drift closer? Did he stare in confusion at a kindness so unexpected?

Nana extends her hands to offer the bleeding creature a cloth.

The man crumples. She rushes forward, keeps him from falling.

"I've got you," she whispers. "Hold on."

"I don't know if I can."

"You can."

Is the "ungodly howl" Dom later describes the shriek of an approaching police car or ambulance? Was Dom disoriented, woozy from the impact of the crash and simply mistaken? I think not. I believe the sound was something more, a howl of defeat, a cry of the damned, the screech of the gates of Hell yawning.

I believe it was the Pale Man.

Chapter 75

We gathered by the hundreds in New Hope Cemetery. So many familiar faces, newcomers too, standing against the swift tides of change and dissolution to embrace the blessings of community and to embrace a town—"like so many small towns"—where hope could flourish.

Joe and Steve Adams represented not just the best of us but all of us. Alice Watters made that clear, bringing generations of parents and students together in laughter and tears. Never had New Hope witnessed such an outpouring. We'd come to say farewell, but their absence made their lives, their decency, burn brighter.

Like Nana, they would live on as symbols of tragedy and triumph that make the lives of ordinary people ("the Word made flesh") extraordinary to others.

After all, is this not our purpose under heaven?

In the years ahead, Nana and I prayed together. We talked about what I now retell in this story. She wanted to know if such extraordinary events were possible or just the dreams and imaginings of an old woman. She wanted to believe that Jack had kept his promise.

"Is it possible, Pastor?"

I searched long for the right words. I told her I believed that sometimes, with God's grace, spirits can reach across the great divide that holds them separate and apart from those they love. These spirits can comfort us and show there is a greater power for good than we mortals, no matter how strong our faith, can know. Jack Martin had loved Nana. She was his beloved wife. In the next world, I believe he loved her still but now in the service of a Greater Love. This was his heavenly purpose. And Jack, or what Jack had tried so hard to teach his family, did not fail.

I remember the service clearly. It was my time to speak. I've always been a man who cries easily, and I can still hear the sobs echoing and reverberating in the chill air. I recall the mourners drawing together, their ranks closing into a circle that grew ever tighter and stronger until it was invulnerable to harm.

There was Dom Palermo holding Nicky's mittened hand and, next to him, DJ and Sally, their bright future ahead of them. Dorrie Smith, hatless in the snow, stood next to them. How fierce she was, this last leaf of a family tree that had taken root in New Hope two hundred years ago. Who would have believed she'd rouse herself again, use her newfound skills and become once again a driving force for combating ignorance and, yes, ambivalence?

I saw Sam and Rose Stone. The physician's rage against the dying of the light was now softened by a deeper, more intuitive knowledge that science and faith are inextricably linked on the long chain of human experience. He'd fought so ferociously for all his patients. He'd do the same for Nana and so many others.

I looked at Nana. She stood next to Jane, so tall, her sheltering arms around her daughters. I sensed joy in Nana's heart and knew that she'd found the peace that had so long eluded her.

I saw something else too, something that fills me with dread and wonder to this day. By God's grace I believe I saw Jack Martin. I think Sam Stone saw him too, though it was not something we would ever talk about.

He stood there, a figure radiating pure white light, alongside his beloved. He smiled at me, and my words caught in my throat. I felt the hand of God upon me. And such joy! Such joy. I knew that Jack's promise had been fulfilled.

I looked down. The light was blinding ... like cold fire. And in that glow ... was George.

Epilogue

Yes, I sensed the Pale Man lurking in the trees below us. I imagine he dared not approach our blessed circle. Rebuffed, he would move on to another place, another town, and another season to spread his poison. Marshalling his power, probing for weakness, always stronger and more determined.

Among the first words I wrote were, "You wouldn't remember New Hope." This, too, is the Pale Man's work. Forgetfulness. All these years I've watched and waited, never forgetting. With this tale, my burden is lifted. Let others be watchful.

I've delivered the message. My task is done. It is for you to find the goodness and strength in your heart to build community, embrace faith and charity, and in doing so, carry on the Lord's work.

For the Pale Man lurks ever outside your door.